JANE FRASER lives, works and writes fiction in Gower in a house facing the sea. By day she is co-director of NB:Design along with her husband, Philip. In 2017 she was a finalist for the Manchester Fiction Prize. In 2018 she was placed second in the Fish Memoir Prize and selected as one of Hay Writers at Work. She has a PhD in Creative Writing from Swansea University.

THE SOUTH WESTERLIES

JANE FRASER

SALT

CROMER

PUBLISHED BY SALT PUBLISHING 2019

4 6 8 10 9 7 5 3

Copyright © Jane Fraser, 2019

Jane Fraser has asserted her right under the Copyright, Designs and Patents Act
1988 to be identified as the editor of this work.

First published in Great Britain in 2019 by
Salt Publishing Ltd
12 Norwich Road, Cromer, Norfolk NR27 0AX United Kingdom

www.saltpublishing.com

Salt Publishing Limited Reg. No. 5293401

A CIP catalogue record for this book is available from the British Library

ISBN 978 1 78463 195 6 (Paperback edition)
ISBN 978 1 78463 196 3 (Electronic edition)

Typeset in Neacademia by Salt Publishing

Printed and bound in Great Britain by Clays Ltd, Elcograf S.p.A

To my husband, Philip, for his encouragement and unfaltering belief in me, my three granddaughters, Megan, Florence, and Alice, for the joy they bring every passing day, and to the memory of the late Welsh poet, psychogeographer, academic, and man of Gower, Nigel Jenkins.

CONTENTS

THE SOUTH WESTERLIES

THIS IS THE BOAT
THAT DAD BUILT

RAYMOND WILLIAMS THE butcher rises every day at 6 o'clock sharp. Above the shop he swings his legs over the edge of the bed onto the threadbare carpet as soundlessly as he can. He doesn't want to wake Mum, still sleeping deeply now as morning comes; she needs her rest. He pads in his slippers past the bedroom of us, his two children, Jane and Peter, and descends the steep stairs with a young man's tread, the wedding ring on his fourth finger tapping against the varnished banister. He'll bring us a cup of tea and a biscuit in an hour or so; no need to disturb us yet, let us come-to gently, drift easily into the day. Till then he'll chop: the rhythmic plodding thud of his life, marking time, Monday to Saturday, cutting grooves into the already worn surface of the wooden block that bows in the centre with the weight of the heavy years.

Dad made his vows ten years earlier on a Monday morning in June soon after the Coronation. And he meant them. *Till death us do part; forsaking all others as long as ye both shall live.* He doesn't want a lot out of life; he's easily pleased, content with his lot. Then again, perhaps that's the problem. Not that Mum acknowledges there's a problem. It's just her nerves, she says – can't seem to sleep at night, feels constantly *low*. She often talks of things past, of the *good* clothes she used to have when she was growing up, from fashionable department stores like Ben Evans or Sydney Heath's in the Swansea town centre. And she talks endlessly about Martin who's a dentist now in middle-class shore-line Mumbles. She *could have had this*; she *could have had that*. But she chose Dad, the red-headed man she spied on the beach at Langland soon after the sands were free again at the end of the war.

But for now she goes for a lie down every afternoon as life continues to play out in the terraced streets around her. The flimsy peach curtains are drawn in the dim bedroom, the eiderdown pulled up tightly to her chin, her breathing as rhythmic as the chopping below. Her silent dreams are taking her where Dad can only guess, away from the hollow depression she'll leave in the feather mattress when she gets up.

"Where's Mum?" I demand as soon as I get in from school and pass through the shop where my father stands, still chopping at his block.

"In bed. Having a little lie down," he replies.

"It's not fair. Why is she always in bed?"

Dad says nothing as he chops on. Our eyes meet for a second in my reflection in the mirror behind the block as I pass by. I disappear into the back of the house which lies achingly empty at the end of the afternoon.

Much later, when Mum finally leaves the shuttered fug of the bedroom and comes downstairs, it's obvious she senses my feeling of resentment and abandonment. She is gagging on her guilt but fends off the uneasiness bittering her mouth by going on the attack. She tells me that I am a *moaner*, that I was born moaning probably because I was a forceps delivery. *Wednesday's child is full of woe*, she tells me, which doesn't seem fair either.

Dad never takes my side. His blind patience infuriates me.

"Look Jane, don't go upsetting your mother now – saying nothing's best. You know she needs her rest and likes a little lie down in the afternoons. She's a bit down at the minute."

I don't know why she needs her rest. I just know it's different; this strange house where my mother is neither present nor absent, hidden behind the façade of the shop window where the sheets of greaseproof paper hang on steel hooks at the end of each day and close us off from the pavement and the rest of the world.

But Mum, at times, seems on Dad's side, as though she has admiration for his certain *type* of skills.

"He's good with his hands," she tells us from on high, "very practical, methodical. Of course, he didn't have much of an education – wasn't allowed to – had to come out of Dynevor Grammar School at fourteen and help out in the shop because of the war and all that. So he's not a great reader, more a non-fiction man."

Yes, that's true; the only point of reading as far as he is concerned is for facts. So it's *Amateur Photography* or *Woodwork Today*. He's not a fiction lover like Mum, though he loves to sing and soar away on Welsh hymns. But it is around this time that he stops singing in the Morriston Orpheus Choir because Mum is becoming tired of him going to choir practice twice a week. She says it's just the fact that she's left alone in the evenings with nothing to occupy her but the children. He doesn't want to upset her even more so he accommodates. Yes, that's the word for Dad; accommodating. And so when the music leaves his soul he embarks on a once-a-week woodwork course, on a Monday evening.

"It's not fair, Dad," I say. "Why do you always give in

to Mum, always let her have her own way? You love your singing – you should tell her!"

"Look Jane, your mother hasn't had an easy life, what with one thing and the other – there's no point making things worse – it's just not worth it, it's not that important. And anyway, I've been fancying turning my hand to a bit of wood-work for a while now."

There's a look of obedient dog about him; a dog that keeps running after thin twigs and sticks chucked by his mistress on a cold, deserted beach – a dog that keeps running back, crouching, begging for more until he's panting and his legs won't carry him anymore. A dog who doesn't want to give up or cause displeasure.

But the woodwork times are solid times – hardwood in our family. He works in jarrah and karri and fruitwood and mahogany. He brings the exotic to the back of the shop. He planes and joints and bevels and turns grained planks into an array of wonderful creations which adorn the place: delicate light-pulls for the bathroom, fine-turned lamp bases for the living room, a teak desk with a knee hole for me to do my homework, a garage with petrol pumps and even ramps and a sign painted red, *Pete's Motors*, for my brother. And for Mum, a lustrous, mahogany bedside cabinet which feels like satin, but is solid and heavy, made to last. It glows warm red with a brass-encrusted handle that glitters like gold and a drawer that glides with a whisper because of his perfect dove-tailing.

It's then he decides he'll build the boat. The boat that will spirit us all away from the terraces of Swansea east. And in the short precious times that are available to us on Saturday afternoons and Sundays, he will be Neptune, King of all he surveys, at the helm. With his family all together on board they will skim the safe waters, not too far from shore, but all at sea. He smells the dream.

And the dream takes shape in the unused bedroom above the shop at the front of the house. His crew is already all on board. Meticulously, he works from a plan: *build your own 11-foot dinghy*. The step-by-step guide lies open on the wooden floorboards and he's dressed in his brown button-through cotton overall that replaces his butcher's apron, when the steam of the Morphy Richards electric kettle eases the carefully sawn strips of wood into shape, and they bring flesh to the bones as he moulds them carefully around the ribs of the skeleton of the framework.

The dream starts to become visible.

"It's coming, Ray, taking shape," Mum purrs, as though she wants to be on board for the first time in her life.

"You're so clever Dad . . . how long till it's finished?" we kids say together.

And we are allowed to mix the glue that is thick and strong, the heady-smelling adhesive that will hold the wood in place, make it safe and watertight before we brush on the undercoat and the final varnish on the prow.

"She's a beauty," says Mum. "I'm really looking forward to summer."

And for the first time in his life Dad must feel something akin to pride, coursing through his industrious veins. And as the long winter nights start to shorten and spring wafts in through the open sash window, turps and thinners and plywood and paint and brushes and balsa and varnish and vanity and excitement and expectation choke the air. The boat is complete.

5

Mum brings tea in the four best blue-and-white-striped china mugs on a tray for the ceremony. We all eat Marie biscuits in the early ethereal evening light. It is then, with great seriousness and dignity, that Dad, in his best BBC English, christens his dream:

"I name this boat, JAPET. May God bless her and all who sail in her."

And he means it, really means it. Dad who is so earnest, who has such hope and optimism. Logically, as expected, in his matter-of-fact sort of way, he takes two syllables and melds them together with love. He takes his children's names and marries them in a flourish of gold seraph-face lettering and fixes them securely with brass screws to the prow of his boat. His whole world is reflected.

It is side-splitting when the great crafter of dreams realises that his creation is too big to leave the room by normal means. The dream has outgrown the physical context; it is more of a liner than a dinghy. It is confined to quarters for a while as he works out how to resolve the situation. Another small trial sent to test him. All part of life's rich plan, he thinks.

But soon after, a sense of sadness, perhaps even shame, sweeps over me as I see my father's visions all dangling in chains above the pavement where Evan the Milk's ageing milk float will soon receive it, in the back space where the milk crates have been cleared. The window frame is taken out and it's just there, JAPET, swinging like a dead man on a gibbet. I feel my face redden with embarrassment or perhaps a sense of things to come. I am too young to understand fully; but some feeling sends my emotions into overdrive.

"Stop being so over-dramatic, Jane. See the funny side," says my mother. That's not fair, I think, coming from her.

This is the time when fairness is something solid, tangible. Something you can feel in your hands like the white Avery scales on the counter in the shop below. The time when everything equates; balances up. When good things happen to good people, when good people don't die young, when hard work results in rich rewards – when the more you give, the more you receive, the more you love, the more you are loved. You know the sort of time. The time I see my father's boat, my father's pride, being mocked by things as yet unseen, undefined.

We don't have a trailer to ferry the boat back and fore to the beach – can't afford one – so JAPET is housed permanently at Oxwich Bay. Dad comes to an arrangement with a local land owner, a Sir Charles Stuart something-or-other, who has an estate where the woods nestle up to the Old Rectory and run right down to the shore line tucked away at the eastern corner of the bay next to the church at St Illtyd's.

"She'll be safe as houses there," he says confidently. "Even have God looking out for her!"

It is probably then that I, like my mother, see the ordinariness of our little dinghy which has been until then, wondrous. It is not lustrous and fibre-glassed, replete with visors and padded leather seats like the others that flaunt themselves in the bay. *Vulgar*, Mum says they are, *new-moneyed*, tersely, her full lips suddenly drawing in, thinning. I sense it is the kind the dentist I have heard about would probably have now. Our JAPET is a mere eleven foot. It doesn't have a Mercury 200HP outboard engine that cuts through the water nor does it bounce at speed leaving a great wake of white water behind. JAPET has a 2-stroke engine which leaves a rainbow of smelly oil behind as it chugs diligently across the bay, out from the corner of the beach that loses the sun in the afternoon, out into the open sea towards the steep limestone cliffs, glinting in the beckoning sunlight at Tor Bay.

It is another world, out there away from the shore. We are free, unfettered on the calm and open sea. We sing in unison, 'Life on the Ocean Wave' or 'We All Live in a Yellow Submarine' over and over again because our new life jackets are yellow; fluorescent-yellow life jackets that lace up at the front and have sharp edges but will keep us buoyant and free from danger. And when the engine is cut and we jump overboard, we bob like light cork in the fish-filled water. And Mum's bather is yellow too; two-toned, an acid yellow and a darker hue, more mellow, smudging together in circles like the sun and a halter neck, a boned bodice and a skirt like a tutu that skims the top of her thighs. And with her rimless sunglasses with the golden metallic wings she is a starlet from a Hollywood film set. Though the films are in black and white, she is a technicolour dream.

These are sunshine times, and Dad beams for the dream he has made possible. And I can see him imagining Mum, his starlet, on a mono-ski behind his powerful boat. He has the wheel in one hand and is looking back over his shoulder, the spray salting his face. And she is smiling, her amber eyes sparkling; so confident she is raising her one arm and waving as she carves up the ocean. We kids are screaming with joy on the pretend padded leather seats as the boat smacks and slaps on the surface. We bounce up and down as he steers us at speed fearlessly across the bay. In the distance, at the far end of the wide sweep of limestone coastline, the afternoon sunshine looks even brighter, its warmth drawing us towards it. But perhaps he thinks we are sailing a little too close to the sun and the dreams are starting to melt when the 2-stroke engine cuts out and there is a silence. We row back to shore then, our arms aching, back to the safe haven of the trees next to the church, our home-made oars, varnished with love, slicing and shining through the water, rhythmically keeping time to the gentle chant of the skipper.

Summer is passing. The first chill days of autumn are about to descend, the leaves to fall off the trees. Mum does not want to go out in the boat anymore.

"It's getting a bit cold for me, Ray – you go with the kids. I'll stay on the shore."

And there she sits on the red and green striped beach towel on the cool damp sand at the water's edge. She's smiling and waving at us as JAPET, sounding now like a sewing machine, splutters into life and stutters across the bay, fading into the distance, bathed in that low glow of late September light.

Dad must sense Mum fading too. No more a Hollywood starlet, her screen days are over and she's feeling the chill again, already wrapped tightly in Dad's worn tweed sports jacket and a headscarf and sipping tea from a red Thermos flask, alone on the shore.

It is the time when the season comes to an end with a sudden storm. A rise of the wind, an eerie omen that precedes the tempest; fork lightning, torrents of rain – a complete cataclysm. They say it is spectacular, the people in Oxwich who see it play out over the bay, the sea a deep plum-purple, unfathomable.

But of course, we aren't there to witness it; we're back in Swansea east. We get a call about a day later from the Old Rectory – we need to come down, it's not good news. Sir Charles Stuart something-or-other hasn't bothered to manage these woodlands at the estate's edge for years. You can see that the trees are dry, desiccated, brittle. It's no wonder they split. I know that God has done this on purpose.

They say nothing, Mum and Dad, as they lift the trunk off the smashed hull. The split is perfectly symmetrically, right down the middle. It must have been one mighty strike, a mighty smite. The engine is bent and buckled; useless. And all Dad's love and labour is litter now, chips and chunks on the woodland floor. Dad bends and rummages around to retrieve the name, JAPET, still golden among the debris, and rubs it clean on the leg of his trousers. I feel his unshed tears well-up inside me festering in a fierce anger against something or someone; but he remains his calm self as he stands there with his two children at his side.

"Oh well, at least not everything's lost," he says.

And Mum says nothing, just stands apart, before walking off through the leafless trees.

There is a feel of the coming winter.

A PASSING FRONT

T HINGS WERE NEVER the same after she'd left that late September day. I'd expected autumn storms to sweep in off the Atlantic, just as they always did: south-westerly squalls that would wipe summer clean away, once and for all. But that year, they didn't come.

The Indian summer hung on like my wife's long and lingering presence. Well into October, the garden groaned with an abundance of growth: yellow roses still bloomed, clinging to the old stone wall of the shed, filling the air with sweetness. Strawberries cropped a second time, overflowing from the warmth of the terracotta tubs and climbing beans and courgettes choked the raised beds. And from the gnarled, old apple tree that she loved, hung boughs, heavy with the weight of Nutmeg Pippins, begging to be picked. But I just didn't have the inclination.

Of course, the days were shorter come November, and relatively cooler, but the sun insisted on shining still. Its rays slanted through the branches of the apple tree, creating a shimmering, dappled light. Leaves, usually long-gone, clung bravely to the twisted branches, along with the odd apple. I should have started tidying-up, I suppose, looking back: getting things in order, ready for the winter, but it didn't feel as though winter would come that year. *It's not natural, this,* my old dad kept muttering, as he came and tried to take control of the garden, *even the grass is still growing.* I felt helpless to help him, my father. *There, there,* he said softly, as if I were a child again, *it'll come, boy.*

Under the balding canopy of the tree, the glut of unpicked apples lay on the grass. In the cool of dawn, and just before dusk descended, I would watch a lone magpie bobbing its ugly monochrome head in a monotonous rhythm, spearing its thieving, jet beak through the skin of the abandoned fruit and gouging its way into the exposed flesh, ripe beneath the surface. Deeper and deeper it would dig, until it would have its fill. And then it would just take flight.

The harvest of apples just lay rotting. Daily I'd tread along the slippery, moss-covered path that skirted that tree and notice that the fruit was shrinking, putrefying. The skin that hadn't been picked and gnawed by birds was brown and the fruit inside soft, pulpy. The heady waft of sweet-decay filled the air and attracted swarms of wasps that hovered, circling, inches above the rotten apple flesh. They seemed half asleep or drugged; high on this late bounty. They were strangely hypnotic circling this way, desperate to taste of the last fruits of summer.

But in December, the first frost came down. It bit hard. I'd been lulled into a false sense of security by the magic trickery of a summer I thought would never end. Overnight the garden was transformed; and I ventured out incredulous at how rapidly appearances could change. Under the fragile white frosting, all evidence of what had once been, had been covered up, hidden under this flimsy blanket. The world was stripped of colour; and I retreated indoors, to the warmth, away from the sudden shiver of winter.

The conservatory had been her idea so that even at that point in my life I had to acknowledge she'd been right. It took advantage of every ray of sun from its rise over the Bulwark behind the house, to its fall into the ocean out front.

Winter's blast might have made itself felt outside, but inside, in the conservatory, I was warmed through, snug and secure in my room of glass. Always light and hot, that even without central heating I'd have to open up the sash windows to let in some fresh air.

It must have been then that the first of the wasps found its way in; tempted by this easy warmth, away from the sudden and inhospitable chill outside. But once inside, it must have sensed that getting out would be more difficult. After a few minutes buzzing over the fruit bowl, it found itself trapped behind the glass. It was a frenzy of transparent vibrating wings, flying into the windows, disorientated and agitated, its tiny black and yellow thorax beating against the pane, its antennae feeling this barrier to escape, over and over again, as it pounded against the glass, perhaps sensing its own futility.

I didn't have the heart to kill it myself, though perhaps it would have been wise to put it out of its misery there and then. Instead, I rolled up a recent edition of *Business in Focus* that was lying in the magazine rack and, at first, tried to gently flick the stranded wasp towards the open windows. But it seemed to resist my good intentions to let it fly free. I opened the floor-to-ceiling double-glazed patio doors and banged on the glass with the pages, hoping to frighten it out. I meant it no harm; but its two domed eyes blindly refused to see a way out. It merely buzzed louder and louder at a higher pitch, I thought, and at an increased volume. It continued in this frenzied mode, until its will to live petered out. It just stopped trying, and slowly the noise, which was getting right inside my head by then, abated. The crazed wasp settled on the slate floor inches from the escape route I'd offered, and just lay there.

I didn't know that much about wasps; but I'd heard that when they were in this semi-conscious state, they were at their most aggressive and were most likely to sting, if danger threatened. I inched nearer, still clutching my cylinder of paper intent on nudging it out. It sensed my approach and issued a kind of last gasp buzz. So I let it lie. I would let it die naturally, without interference, though I was at no time afraid of a possible sting. I felt immune.

It was where I'd left it when I came downstairs the following morning; very still then, very much dead, its six jointed legs, stiff and brittle. For some unexplained reason, although I'd always hated wasps, I didn't like to see it dead. I somehow thought it was all my fault; if I hadn't had the window open, it wouldn't have sneaked in and died. But then again, wasps in December? It just wasn't natural. Methodically, I went to the utility room cupboard and got the dust pan and brush and gently swept it up into the body of the pan. There would have been a time in my life when I would simply have hurled it into the wind; but I felt inexplicably sad and I felt my face wet with tears.

I picked up the dead little body and laid it down in one of her old *Russell and Bromley* shoe-boxes that I'd been clearing and intending to sling out. It looked lost inside the cavernous cardboard space, but I decided that I'd keep it in there nevertheless, safe and stored, as my daughter had done with her nail clippings when she was a young and compulsive child. She just simply couldn't bear to part with them. Now, nor could I, this wasp. I closed the lid and secreted the box in the corner of the conservatory, tucked in at the side of the wine rack. Looking back, I suppose I was keeping the box, at the ready, as if I was to expect more.

And I was right. As the cold snap continued, the wasps were drawn inside, at first singly and then in pairs. Two became four became eight became more. I felt I was luring them towards their death, that I'd be responsible for their ending, that I'd always be responsible for evermore. There were times when the buzz became unbearable as they flew close to my head; though they never touched me, never attempted to sting. I tried my hardest not to kill them. I tried my hardest for them not to kill themselves. Though if I am honest, there were times when I'd misjudge the impact of my rolled-up magazine and perhaps I must have stunned one or two by accident in my attempt to gently coax them out. I'd watch their dying bodies twitch and writhe on the slate floor, but I still couldn't deliver the decisive blow.

It didn't take long for a thin layer of dead insects to completely crust the base of the shoe box. Some were not whole as they once had been, they'd lost a leg, or a wing, or perhaps an antenna in the frenzy of death. I was quite upset by these detached body parts, and I was longing for this invasion of wasps in December to cease.

When it did, it was the noise I missed first. A sudden stillness filled the house and deafened me, the sort of stillness you hear when the electricity fails, when the familiar whirr of the freezer becomes conspicuous by its absence. I'd become used to their intrusive buzz, it was normal. Perhaps I even missed it; the house was so empty and silent now the noise had gone.

It was probably down to the weather. There'd been a sudden rise in temperature, a mild front had come in off the ocean; a big low-pressure system which hung heavily over south Wales. I'd watched the tightly-packed isobars on the weather forecast after the six o'clock news. It was a 992. It was murky, just grey Welsh drizzle, fine misty rain, and it seemed we wouldn't be having a white Christmas after all.

With the rain, came my wife, just days before Christmas. She stood at the conservatory door wearing her mac and a tentative smile. She stood with her bag in her hand on the very spot she'd said goodbye, just twelve weeks earlier. She'd been crying by the look of her: her eyes were red and puffy – she'd never been a pretty crier. It hadn't worked out apparently. She'd made a huge mistake and she was so sorry to have hurt me, to have put me through so much and was I OK, and could she come back, give it one more try over Christmas?

I didn't like to say no to her as she stood there soaked through by the drizzle, seeking the warmth and comfort of what once had been her conservatory. I helped her with her heavy load up the familiar stairs to the room we'd once shared. I felt the waft of time passing brush me on the forearm. I felt disoriented and out of kilter. I thought how those wasps must have felt. I noticed she smelled different. It wasn't the perfume she'd always worn when we were married. It was a fruitier smell, heady, a smell of warm summer evenings. The scent hung in the air as I went back downstairs, back to the conservatory. I told her to make herself at home, settle herself down and I'd be up later. I had a few things to sort out downstairs.

It was dark then. December dark. Darkness and drizzle were pressing in from the outside, heavy against the undressed windows of the conservatory, which were pulled down then, tight, fixed, keeping everything out. In the silence, by the light of my reading lamp, I opened up the shoe box which I'd since labelled: FRAGILE – DECEMBER WASPS – KEEP OUT. I spread a large sheet of baking parchment over the large polished table. It brightened the light, reflected it back into my face, now bleached white. I'd only need the tweezers and the Airfix glue, which I placed neatly on the sheet, in readiness. The dead wasps – some whole, some segmented into thorax, stalk and abdomen, some with and some without wings and what seemed like hundreds of minute black, thread-like joints, formed a crispy heap in the centre of the parchment.

Although the light was perfect and I could see with such clarity, I didn't know where to begin in my mission to put them together again, make them whole. I worked with earnestness, trying to undo what I had done, repair what I'd torn apart. The tweezers trembled in my right hand as I delicately selected the odd transparent wing, and one by one tried to assemble it in position with the prongs of the tweezers at exactly the right point where it had become severed from the main body. With my left hand, I squeezed the glue gently through the nozzle of the tube, desperately trying to stick the broken parts together, in the way I'd done as a boy when I'd built all those model planes from the Airfix kit. I'd never had trouble in those days. I felt my father behind me: *That's right. Steady hand. Plenty of patience. That'll do it.*

But that was then. Now I wasn't achieving the desired results, no matter how hard I tried to steady my hands. The insects were dried and cracked, some crumbled between my thumb and index finger. I couldn't make out the mandibles or tell the difference between compound eyes and simple eyes and I couldn't find six jointed legs for each abdomen; some lay limbless, other legs looked crooked, pieced together at odd angles, trochanters, tibias and femurs going off at odd tangents. They did not look as they were supposed to; not as they had been once, these poor, once sociable, yellow jacketed arthropods.

I lost track of the time. I don't know how many hours I'd sat there concentrating, trying my hardest through that just-before-Christmas night, by the sickly glare of the light, to put everything right. I just couldn't tell. But she was suddenly there, behind me, her hand touching my shoulder as she'd always done in the time back then, the time before she took flight. I knew her peculiar touch, gentle, yet demanding:

"I thought you said you were coming up, that you wouldn't be long?"

"There was something I had to do first, something I had to put right," I whispered.

My voice sounded different to me; flat, monotone. Though hers sounded just the same.

And it was then she saw the filth of desiccated wasps lying dead in the centre of the parchment.

"But unfortunately it can't be done," I whispered, "it's just not possible."

I must have remained there at the table locked in that same position all night, staring at the heap of death that littered the space in front of me without being able to do anything about it.

And in the morning, she'd gone away again, along with the rain. The front had passed through, and behind it on the horizon appeared a small patch of blue.

OUT OF SEASON

THIS MORNING IT'S just you and the dog in the bus shelter. At seven o'clock on Christmas Day there are no buses, no one waiting. But here in this village by the sea, you seem to have been waiting for something to turn up for a long time. And this morning you're waiting for her. In the pub last night she said she would come.

You sit on the slatted wooden bench inside, out of the drizzle. It's not cold, just dank, Gower dank. Fine misty rain and a light onshore breeze, like most other days. With your right trainer you toe out a capital J in the sand that's blown in across the concrete, banking up in the far corner along with the empty crisp packets and buckled cans. You consider whether you should have etched the initial in lower case. You don't know what your name stands for anymore. Jamie. It might be that it's the vat of Strongbow you downed after you shut up the bar in The Ship last night, but the reek in the shelter seems stronger this morning: the tang of piss, stale cigarette smoke and wet sheep getting to the back of your throat. Fag butts and pellets of shit litter the floor in this space that you've used as many a thing in your time: a refuge, a youth club, a bar, a drug den, a sex shop, whatever was needed when there were things that needed doing and there was nowhere else to go. Like the sheep, you've used it simply to wait for it to stop raining, or just to wait for you don't know what, that might have been just around the corner; though never a bus. But you're twenty-five now and you seem to be the only one left who's still hanging around waiting for something to happen.

You pull your hoodie further over your forehead, tug the fabric at the sides together as far as you can to cover your cheeks and knot it tightly under your chin. Any more and you could disappear. You wonder whether your mum and dad will notice you're not there when they get up. They've got used to letting you sleep it off in the annex. Like a bat, your father says you are: up all night and hanging around almost upside down all day. It's what sloshing about behind the bar does to you. Makes you nocturnal. But today is different and you wonder whether they'll knock on the door later with a cup of tea, come back even later with another cup of tea to replace the one that's gone cold, give you another knock, the final knock, just before they serve lunch. You haven't left a message. No reason really, you just didn't know what you were going to say, what was going to happen.

Out of the mist, you see the lights of her Beetle approaching, on dip, feeble in the dawn that's attempting to break. Even though it's mid-winter and you're the only two souls around, she slows and drives dutifully around the mini-roundabout, indicates, and then pulls up outside the bus stop. You see her face over the distinctive dashboard-mounted flower cup: white sepals, citrus stamens. Briefly, you recall sixth form. She looks washed out. Beautiful but colourless. Everything looks so far away from summer: the ice-cream adverts, the *dim parcio* signs, pay and display car parks, double yellow lines. She presses the electronic button and the driver-side window whirrs down.

"You're risking it pulling up here," you joke. "Better be quick, the warden might be about."

"You came then?" she says. "Get in."

The dog wags its tail and you both take your seats as she indicates again and pulls away out of the village.

Sealed inside the small space with her at the wheel, you suddenly feel uncomfortable, dwarfed. Even though you've known her for almost nine years, ever since she first came wafting onto the school bus with her distinctive flowery smell almost knocking you over, she has this way about her. You worry your breath will still stink of last night's cider, and whether she'll think you are still pissed.

"Is this what I think it is?" you ask. "The final summons?"

"I wanted to talk to you when you're sober, not like you were last night," she says.

"Yeah, like I said, this is it, isn't it?"

She doesn't answer immediately but switches on the demister and the heated rear window and flicks the windscreen wipers to a higher speed. The dog is panting and drooling on the back seat, its breath as rank as yours.

"You've met someone, haven't you?"

"Henry. In clinical."

"Henry. Of course. Never going to be a Jamie, lower case, was it?"

"Sorry?"

"Doesn't matter."

"Look, you know this can't go on. Coming home at the end of term. Stop; start. Stop; start. We're not going anywhere, are we?"

"Me, more like it. Go on. Say it."

She stares ahead, the wipers struggling to clear the screen. The noise of the rubbers is getting to you. You wrench the hoodie, trying to cover even more of your face, and cross your arms tightly over your chest.

It seemed summer would last forever when you were sixteen. Lots of you were earning a wage in The Ship, behind the bar or in the kitchen. It had all been enough. The holiday buzz in Port Eynon was infectious, a heady feeling of freedom and sunshine that would sweep in with the visitors and their expectant faces. There was a security in the rhythm of things: when the summer was over, the caravans would be locked up, the tents taken down, the tourers hitched up ready to go along with the swallows on the wires. You'd go back to Sixth Form College then, until you were needed in the pub when summer came round again.

You didn't really notice your friends, the boys, but mostly the girls, pack up and go off to university. One by one they went, until you were the only one left behind the bar.

In winter when the nights are dark and the customers few, and the rain pours horizontally, it feels a long way away from your youth. There are the farmers, and the pool and too many joints. Apart from that there's nothing much. You just carry on. Every day you look at Brawn, the pub manager, and see yourself thirty years down the line. Once he'd been sixteen and now he's fifty-six, still pulling pints, emptying the ash trays, washing the glasses, stinking of frying and fat and chips, still trying to pull the young girls.

And now your guts are turning over, grumbling loudly in the small territory you're sharing with her. You wish you'd grabbed something to eat before you left the house; some carbs to soak up the booze. There's still a burning acid in your mouth. You place your hand over your stomach and press in the futile hope of quietening the growl. The sight of your coarse and chapped hands affronts you. The silence that has fallen between you heightens the noises your body is making.

You feel the need to vomit, the urge to empty your bowels, as though the whole world is pouring away from you, leaving you a hollowed-out husk.

"Lie down, for fuck's sake, keep still, Celt," you shout at the dog in the back. He shrinks down on all fours and lays his head on his front paws, looking at you with threatened eyes.

She checks the rear-view mirror before signalling right at the folly. You sense the irony in a semi-ruined dwelling of Gower stone, pretending to be a castle keep. It marks the junction of the south Gower road with the steep twisty descent to Oxwich. Your stomach drops in synch with the gradient before the road levels out as it squeezes between the marshes on either side. The waters are milky still, wading birds stalking out their territory between the rushes. She drives you through the head-high reeds. It feels like a long mile to you, enclosed in this strange kind of tunnel. You remember the times when you were a child, the sense of fear and doom you'd feel when your father drove the Astra along here; an irrational fear that the water on either side of the car would rise and swamp you, suck you into its unfathomable depths. You'd sit on the back seat, exactly in the middle, in the hope of escape. And now that feeling is back.

"You still up for this?" she asks as she pulls into the car park.

"Why wouldn't I be?" you say. "It's what we do, isn't it?"

The tide is on the ebb as you unzip your tracksuit. You've got your board shorts on ready underneath. You pick your way barefoot across the pebbles and onto the beach. She's already there ahead of you, waiting with the dog. She's always first to get anywhere, always bristling with enthusiasm. Doesn't seem to feel the cold. She's standing there in her sensible black bather designed for serious swimming, her muscular body planted firm on the sand. She's chucking sticks. *Fetch boy*, she's shouting and your scruffy old mongrel is bounding back and fore, to his would-be mistress, eager to please, doing as he's told. It touches a nerve.

The vast expanse of exposed sand is mud-grey under the low cloud and interminable spits of rain. You're not the only ones here: other swimmers are braving the sea for the traditional Christmas-morning swim and a small crowd has gathered at the water's edge with coffee ready for when they come out. It all looks so ordinary to you when inside your head you realise something extra-ordinary is happening. You are swamped by that out-of-season feeling; a tiredness that you can't sleep off anymore however long you lie in. It is always so grey in Gower, you think, thick grey and sludgier this morning. The sky and the sea are fudged on the horizon, the limestone rocks, steeper; the leaden cliffs at Tor Bay in the distance, nearer. Even the herring gulls look greyer.

"Everything's closing in," you say.

She runs and dives straight under, without fuss, without a gasp for breath. She turns to you and shouts, "Come on, it's not so bad once you're under." You're taking small steps, feeling the water chill your calves, your thighs, your groaning stomach. You flick drops over your shoulders, your chest, your forearms. You notice how pale your limbs are, how they don't seem to see the light of day anymore. You have an image of yourself as a translucent jellyfish stranded on a shoreline, blue-tinged, insides visible to the world. You wonder about Henry's body before you immerse yourself under a wave that's rolling in and hold your breath for as long as you dare.

Beyond the shore break, you swim like synchronised

swimmers towards Three Cliffs. Side by side, you slice through the surface: front crawl, breathing every second stroke, to the left. As you raise your head from the water, you hear the intermittent yap of your dog as it tries to keep up with you, bound for bound along the strandline. In the water, you and her are equally matched, stroke for stroke you keep perfect tempo. You live up to the target she has set you: one mile there, one mile back, until you find yourself once more tucked in the corner of the bay, where the church nestles in the woods that run down to the sea.

Then she disappears beneath the surface and you feel in those few seconds what it's going to be like when she's not around. But then she rises and entwines her legs around your waist, entangles her arms around your neck pressing her face to yours. She kisses you hard, full on the lips. She tastes of salt and toothpaste and seaweed and fresh fish. You will always remember the smell of her. It is only a moment, but long enough for you to read her intentions.

And then you are both back on the beach. You think about quicksand and whether you could be gulped whole. You trudge back to the car, your legs heavy after the exercise. Your dog is shaking madly trying to free himself from the water and sand, and barking, demanding to be let back in the Beetle. She puts a towel for him on the back seat and he lies down. You've brought your own towel, but she's brought black bin liners for you to stand on and a plastic bowl for you to put your sodden board shorts in. You will always remember her practicality. You stand there trembling as you towel dry, feeling the need to get your hoodie on again sharpish, to pull those drawstrings tight. You get back in her car and she switches on the ignition and blasts the heater.

The front is slowly passing through; but your mood does not lift. You don't want to talk, you say. Nothing much to say anymore. You're just a boy with a name that's best spelled out in lower case. You're not even capable or rich enough to drop out anymore, especially in Gower. You're just a drop-in, really. A twenty-five-year-old drop-in who lives in an annex.

She drives you back into Port Eynon, down the steep hill, past the church with the white stone statue put up in honour of men lost at sea, past the chip shop with the steel shutters pulled down, past the run-down restaurant with the wind-torn adverts, on past The Ship that won't be open until tomorrow.

"D'you want me to take you home, come back with you for a while?" she asks.

"No, it's alright, just drop me off at the bus shelter. I'll manage to make my own way from there."

CHRISTMAS CRACKERS

M UM'S IN THE car waiting for me outside High
Street Station. I told her I'd be getting the 19:00 from
Paddington rather than driving back as it was the office Christmas party. She didn't seem to mind, but asked if I'd feel a bit
stuck without the car while I was home and that I couldn't rely
on her to ferry me around like she used to as she was working
now, remember?

It's raining, not heavy, but fine drizzle that reminds me
I'm home. She gets out and hugs me, that distinctive smell
enveloping me. Mummy smell, I call it. I can conjure it up
on demand: all through the years I was in university and
even now when I'm supposed to be a grown-up living in
London.

I go to the boot to put my case in, but she tells me I'll
have to put it on the back seat as the boot's full of books. I
still see her in her little grey BMW. It's easy to forget how
things have changed when you're away, perhaps to choose to
forget that she's a book rep now and drives this red Astra up
and down the motorway every day. In the glare of the street
lights, she no longer looks as I remember. We used to be told
we looked like sisters.

"You've had a few," she remarks. "Enjoy?"

"Good, thanks," I reply guiltily.

"Rob get off alright?"

"Yeah, he texted me to say he'd arrived. His mum and dad
were driving down to Sydney to pick him up."

"That's nice – you'll miss him over Christmas, I bet?"

"Be alright. Catch up with everyone."

"You going to see your father, then?"

I wondered how long it would take her to ask.

"Probably," I say.

She doesn't say anything in reply. Not yet, anyway, as we pull out of the car park for the journey home.

I'm still half-cut despite the strain of the initial effort, and in the front seat, feeling safe, with Mum at the wheel, the heater on, and the windscreen swishing, it's difficult to stay awake. I feel I know where I am, even with my eyes closed: the stop-starts at the lights in Uplands, Sketty, Killay, the vibration of the cattle grid at Upper Killay.

"Crossing the border now," Mum says as we do. She has always said this, over all the years she has driven me and my brother back and forth to school in Swansea.

"I know, Mum," I say. "Haven't forgotten."

The click of the indicator means we are onto the North Road and on over Fairwood Common. She picks up speed, though it doesn't feel as fast as it used to: her foot is hovering over the brake, not pressing, but just above, just in case. She never used to care. I feel her slow right down: cows on the road, she says.

I don't have to be told what to do but open the window and bang the side of the car with my hand as the cattle lumber back onto the grass. I wonder what my work colleagues would think if they saw this side of me. Or what they would think if they saw the sheep I'm seeing, trying to keep dry as we pass the bus shelter in Burry Green.

"Bet you'll be glad to get in?" Mum asks. "Almost there."

We wind through the lanes and then slow as we almost

free-wheel down the steep hill into the village. She indicates left.

"I'll do the gate," I say.

I lift the heavy iron contraption that Dad had made to secure the double gates together at the top. The bolt hadn't been enough to stop the horses heaving it open and clomping across the concrete. They'd find their way on to the manicured lawn and hoof it up, leaving shit everywhere. Dad always seemed to be shovelling shit. But even this innovative device had not deterred one wild piebald who'd devised a knack of lifting it with its teeth. As I push the gate open, I can see that horse's piano-key teeth, the loose, euthymol-pink gums. I can see it again from the back window of the house, stiff as death, being clawed off the ground by the blade of a JCB, hoisted high into the air and then flung into a pit dug in the field. I can see it slowly disappearing, covered over, scoop by scoop, with heavy soil. I feel suddenly a long way away from SW3.

There's the goldfish pond in the centre of the drive where one winter the fish froze solid in blocks of ice. The winter of '81, when we were cut off for days because of the snow and the power went and the pipes froze and we all slept downstairs in front of the fire. But it wasn't enough to thaw the tension between Mum and Dad. And there are our footprints, mine and my brother's, cast in concrete outside the house we've both outgrown.

"I'm going straight up if that's OK, Mum. Thanks for picking me up. See you in the morning," I say.

"Lovely to have you home. Perhaps we can do something nice tomorrow, just you and me, like we used to?"

※

My room is just as I left it: all done out in Laura Ashley wallpaper, curtains and patchwork quilt. So much pink, a pair of satin pink ballet slippers hanging off the dressing-table mirror along with a squashy rubber mask of Michael Jackson. I remember Dad driving me and Natalie Rushton up to the Arms Park for the concert. I sit on the bed and it creaks loudly, the wooden head-board posts not quite fitting the slatted base properly. The creaking brings back Rhys Jones, and how I shagged him for the first time in this little single bed of mine when Mum was out. Dad had left by then and I'd just started saving my nail clippings in a Swan Vesta match-box which I kept in the dressing-table drawer. I did that for years: wanting to hang on to them, not being able to bear the thought of letting them go. It stopped for a while, but when Rhys Jones left me for someone he'd met on friendsreunited. com when I left for university, it started up again. I suppose if it hadn't been for that website I'd have lived in this village forever and never gone to London, or become a lawyer. I'd never have met Rob.

I put out the bedside lamp and the room is thick dark, and I can hear the murmur of the sea. When I first went to London I couldn't sleep because of the street lights and the incessant drone of traffic and wail of sirens. Now I have trouble getting off to sleep without them. I try to call Rob on the mobile, but there's no signal.

⚛

Mum's already up doing the veg ready for Christmas Day, even though it's only 11 a.m. on Christmas Eve. She's always done this. And she's always worn lipstick from the time she gets out of bed in the morning, as though she's always expecting someone.

"How many have you got coming for dinner, Mum?" I ask as I see the quantities of potatoes, parsnips, swede, sprouts.

"Just the two of us . . . habit, I suppose. Your brother's going *over there* with *him*."

"Yeah, I know. He said."

"Who? Your father? Did *you* get an invite too, then?"

"Yeah, but I said I was coming here and that I'd pop over in the evening."

"How you getting there? I'm not bloody delivering you anymore. I'm done with that. And he's not coming anywhere near here."

"I won't go then if that's what you want."

I can't remember the exact time when Dad became nameless or had a possessive pronoun attributed to him. Probably around the same time as Oxwich became *over there* and his new wife became *that bloody bitch* and his new children became *that lot*. Already I am feeling that so much changes, yet nothing changes at all.

"I hear he's retiring and off to Australia. That bitch, on my bloody pension, eighteen years."

"Leave it, Mum."

"Well, it can't come a day too soon – Australia, I mean – can't bear sharing the same air as him, living in the same hemisphere."

"You never see him now. Cefn Bryn might well as be the Great Dividing Range."

"Yes, I know that. But it's just the thought of him that close, *over there*."

I have a sudden image of a giant Christmas cracker

31

stretching across Cefn Bryn. It is made of red and green foil. In the kitchen in Oxwich, my father takes one end and in the kitchen in Llangennith my mother takes the other. They tug with all their might waiting for the bang and to see who gets the prize. But there is no bang. The cracker merely disintegrates and there in its tattered body is the prize: me, fragmented, a bit here, a bit there. All over the place.

"Why don't you leave that, Mum? Let's go to Cwm Ivy woods and collect fir cones like we used to. I can help you set the table when we get back."

"I thought we'd go later."

"I'm going up the pub later. Emma emailed me last week to say they'd all be there from the village."

"You didn't say."

"I did. In the car. Won't be up there all night."

"Heard that one before. C'mon then. Better get going to get back."

⁂

Mum parks the car in the field near St Madoc's that Gordon Griffiths has set aside for years to get a bit of additional income. It's got an honesty box by the gate. She tells me that Gordon's been had up by the police and he's in court soon. Apparently, he'd gone at a couple of people who hadn't paid with his air gun. Only at their feet, he'd said. But the police weren't having it.

We walk down the steep lane towards the woods. It's only ten minutes from Llangennith but it's a world apart here: colder, damper, the estuary straight ahead and a cold wind in our faces.

"Glad we never bought over here," she says. "North-facing. No light. Your father was right about something."

"Do you ever miss him, Mum?" I ask.

"No. Never. Just the idea of him. Family."

I link arms with her and we open the National Trust gate into the conifers. There is a feeling of all the years rolling into one. It could be anytime. There is just this place: the brown-needled path; the fir cones littering the verge, the large fat ones that you really want, too high, out of reach; Honey, the retriever shaking in the bracken, too timid to walk through the shadowy path. We go our separate ways to fill our bags. In the half-light she looks old and broken as she bends down in her search for Christmas; but at least we are doing something together for the first time in a long while.

As we walk back up the incline with our bags overflowing, she's loosening up a bit, asking questions about me for a change, instead of digging for dirt about *him over there*.

"This Rob, then, is he the one?"

"I think so. But give it time. I haven't known him that long."

"Will you go to Australia to live?"

"Rob loves London. Finds it so near to everywhere."

"What d'you mean?"

"Well, he likes the fact that he can get on a plane and in an hour can be hearing a different language, in a different country. He's not that keen on Australia. Full of Australians."

"And what exactly does he do in the bank?"

"Futures. He's on the Futures Desk at Citigroup."

"I don't do futures," she says and we laugh.

"And Rhys? You ever hear from him?"

"No. Never."

"You really over him. Truth for Mummy?"

"Well and truly," I say.

"Well stay away from him if he's down that pub tonight. Bastard."

Later, I shower and do my hair. There are things I've never got used to in London: the hard water and the lime scale in the iron and kettle. But here my hair is soft. Makes me feel at home for a while. I do my make-up carefully but decide to dress down for the pub. I'm not *not* thinking that Rhys might be there and I'm more than conscious that I want him to see how I've moved on, how I've made good. Want to make him feel that he's the one left in this little village with his little wife. Let him fester. I'd like to tell him about Rob, how handsome he is, how much he earns, how much he cares for me. That we have a future. I call Rob from the landline before I go out. I wish him Happy Christmas as it's already Christmas morning in Sydney. He asks me how I am. How my mother is. If I'm going out. I tell him I'm staying in with my mother, having a quiet evening. Despite Mum vowing not to be my chauffeur, she offers to run me down to the pub as it's spitting with rain again, but insists she's not coming back to pick me up and tells me not to get in the car with anyone who's had a drink. I take the torch. I can sniff out the route between the pub and the house, just like my dear old dead dog, Honey.

From the outside, The King's Head looks just as it always did at Christmas: tinsel in the little windows, coloured lights festooned under the slate roof line, the metal sign swinging in the wind as though in a movie set in the wild west, which I suppose isn't that far off really. I look through the window of the small top bar, kept mostly for locals in summer, but Emma's not there. Even though she's a mother of three she probably doesn't see herself ready for the age group that sups there. I walk through the main bar and there's no sign of her there either, just people I don't know sitting at tables with dogs on leads next to them. That much is new, and I guess they must be taking advantage of the deals that the pub now offers in the Gower stone units at the back. I conclude they're in the zoo, as we used to call it, though in its time it's been known as the surfers' bar, or simply the bottom bar.

I open the door and the smell of chips hits me along with 'And so this is Christmas' which is blaring out of the juke box. Emma's there on this side of the bar now, the only girl among four boys, including Rhys. It is almost as if they've been standing in the same position since I saw them last. None of them have ever moved outside this place my father and my mother called 'the deathbed of ambition.' On that they at least agreed.

"Hey, Katy. Croeso," shouts Emma as she sees me, "what you having?"

I see that they're all drinking the usual.

"Double Dragon, please. Pint."

"That's my girl. Never forget you're Welsh, bach!"

The boys seem shy for some reason and one by one just say: Alright? How you doing, then? Rhys looks uncomfortable and I'm hoping he's squirming inside. He looks tired or perhaps just older. His squint looks more pronounced. He never wore glasses for his like I did for mine. Emma used to say that we were attracted to each other because we couldn't see straight. She might have been right. My mother said she'd seen our end coming before it had even begun.

"How're the kids, Emma?" I ask.

"Off the fucking wall, the three of them. Fucking crazy with Christmas."

"How d'you manage to get out, then?"

"Good as gold, Matthew. He's doing presents. Happy to see the back of me."

"She happy to let you out too, Rhys?" I ask.

He says nothing, but downs his pint and asks me if I want another. I accept, in my most gracious London-mannered way. And keep on accepting for a good few hours as the juke box makes me more and more miserable with every Christmas anthem it spews out.

Emma's more and more tanked up and threatening to *get her tits out* before the end of the night. She's been behind the bar already simulating a blow job on the beer pumps and sliding them up and down between her breasts. It doesn't seem to shock anyone anymore. I thought she would have grown out of it by now.

"Fancy a fag?" Rhys asks.

I follow him outside into the misty rain to stand under the awning that's been put up for smokers. He gives me a Marlboro Light. I haven't had one for years and the smell of it brings everything into sharp focus.

"Sorry things ended up like they did," he says.

"Don't want to hear it now," I say, "too late for all that. Should have been honest, not taken the piss out of me."

"Thought I was holding you back."

"Don't give me that. Me cramping your style, more like it."

"Big mistake."

"Well, suck it up. We all have to get on with stuff."

"You seem happy with what's his name, anyway."

"How do you know?"

"Seen your pictures on Facebook. Good looking bloke, Australian or something, isn't he?"

"Yes. Sydney. Gone home for Christmas."

"Left you on your own, has he?"

"Don't even think about it, Rhys. Some of us at least can be faithful."

"What about a snog for old times? For Christmas? I'll walk you home."

I could let the booze wash the years and the bad memories clean away; I could fuck up in an instant.

"You know you're bloody crackers. Now piss off. Merry Christmas."

৵৯

I don't go back inside. I feel a sudden urge to retch. I look through the window and see the empty glasses stacked up on the bar, Emma the mother holding court, the blokes ogling her. I feel dirty all of a sudden, stale smoke and beer breath on my mac, tainted by Rhys Jones. I feel like I don't belong here anymore and ashamed that I feel like this. I work out the time in Sydney: 3 a.m. here, almost over for him there with his mother and father, all still to get through for me. Still no signal. Bloody Orange. Bloody place.

I trudge up the hill, soaked through. Mum's left the porch light on for me and the door open, but there's no sign of her at this hour. Why would there be? I hang up my coat, take off my wet boots and pad to the sitting room. There's a smell of

Christmas throughout the house: turkey on timed in the oven, wood smoke and fresh pine. She's been sitting by the fire; but now there's little heat left in the thin layer of white ash in the grate. Our pine cones are arranged on the mantelpiece in between some holly she's picked from the hedge outside. No berries though. Not this year. The Norwegian spruce is decorated as it always was with the stuff she's brought down from the attic: white lights, paper lanterns made in school, a fairy with a broken wand, red and gold baubles in which I can see all of the Christmases past. On the hearth, she's placed a glass of sherry and a mince pie for Santa along with my old pillowcase with the stars on. It's still folded down, the top open wide in readiness for the presents.

In the dining room she's set the table the night before, as she always did. Just two settings now, one at each end. The white damask cloth covers the scratches beneath and she has tried to fill the space between where we'll sit with candles and red chrysanthemums and more fir cones which she's sprayed silver: all the paraphernalia of Christmas. She's put crackers, one each, on the white napkins folded into triangles on our side plates. I put it down to too many Double Dragons and the Marlboro Lights, but I am heaving and want to vomit. I turn off the light and make for my tiny, single bed with its comforting creak. I reach into the dressing table drawer and rifle in the back for the rough feel of the matchbox, pull it out and look at the nail clippings. I take out the scissors from my manicure set and snip my toenails off both feet. I place the remnants into the box, close it and push it into the darkness at the very back of the drawer.

THE GOWER EXPLORER

G WEDDW, YDW I. A widow, am I. I am a widow.
The taste is unfamiliar on the tongue, whichever one I use; though not altogether unpleasant. He is buried. The mourners gone. I sit at the kitchen table which is littered with half-eaten Welsh cakes and curled-up sandwiches, and roll the sweet-sour syllables around my mouth, trying one after the other, to find the language which fits me better now that he's not here.

Pwy ydw i, nawr? Who am I, now?

I remember my mother telling me in *yr hen iaith*, the old tongue, that you could know who a woman was by the contents of her handbag. I open the brass clasp of the only one I've ever had and watch as the contents spill onto the table top: *Order of Service Matthias Joseph Beynon 1928-1998*, a stiffly-starched cotton handkerchief embroidered with G, a plastic comb, hair grips, a brown leather purse, heavy with coins, a house key; and a concessionary bus pass. My image stares back at me from the plastic: unsmiling, empty. There, typed black in bold is Mrs. G. Beynon.

The night seems to slip away without me noticing and when light leaks in, I leave. I don't bother locking the front door but turn and walk away through the yard. The chickens are scratching in the muck, wanting, always wanting; and the brown collies yowl and yelp, straining to break free of their chained leashes; but this morning I leave them to it and make my way to the bus stop.

Dwi'n mynd i deithio. I am going travelling.

The 07:20 116 Gower Explorer pulls up, its distinctive golden daffodil logo yellow against the flat green of the single-decker. I've never been any good with words and numbers when they're written down, in Welsh or English. But I can think and talk and listen along with the best of them.

Dwi'n gallu meddwl a siarad a gwrando.

About half-a-dozen of us board the bus. It's always busy, this one, for the hour commute to Swansea – for those who work. I've never worked in a real job, in a city, anywhere. Just been on the farm. But I've caught this bus alone every Friday for fifty years, shopping bag on my arm, bound for market:

Mynd drot drot ar y gaseg wen
Mynd drot drot i'r dre
Mam yn dod 'nôl dros fryn a dôl
A rhywbeth neis neis i de*

The passengers smile and say Good morning, Mrs. Beynon in the tone that asks without questions: *How do you feel now that Mr. Beynon has gone? How do you actually feel? How are you? Siwd chi'n teimlo?*

How do I feel? I don't know how I feel: strangely elated, angry, frightened, a light weightless sensation of rising, of unfeeling. I won't be drawn. I just want to sit in my usual seat, on the left, three rows from the front and stare out of the window and watch the world that is familiar passing me by.

. . . Llanmadoc . . . Cheriton . . . Oldwalls . . .

It's the usual convoluted stop-start route, picking up passengers outside their garden gates, the end of their lanes. The bus jolts and the gears grind up the inclines and around the hairpin bends along the only road out of this peninsula. I've been told it only takes twenty-five minutes by car. But we never had a car. And if we'd had one, I would never have been allowed to drive. There are a lot of nevers in my life. I count the nevers as we drive through the lanes this March morning: never driven, never read, never written, never had a passport, never had a cheque book, never had children.

Diddiwedd. Never-ending.

. . . Llanrhidian . . .

I don't bother to check my watch: no need now. Don't need to get back for him. *Don't keep a dog and bark yourself,* I hear him say. *Ci,* dog. The words curdling deep in my gut along with the stench of diesel as the bus idles at Llanrhidian. There is nothing that needs doing; but it feels that there is something that always needs doing, a restlessness tugging at me, a widow on the Number 116 to Swansea.

We pull away, skirting the estuary. That's why I sit this side, so that I can gaze out across the water at the mountains tugging me from the other side, *yr ochr arall,* where I came from once upon a time: Carmarthenshire, *Sir Gaerfyrddin.* It seems almost touchable this morning and the *hiraeth,* longing, is churning in my belly. People say that at one time, not so very long ago, there were stepping stones that at low tide connected the land on either side of the Loughor, *Llwchwr.* I used to like to believe it was true and try to imagine myself, on the tide's ebb, picking my away back across the gash of a river that severed me from my roots. And with the tide's flow, the stones would disappear, my escape route covered up, and I'd be in back our farm in Llanddowror, in Carmarthenshire.

. . . Crofty . . . Llanmorlais . . . Penclawdd . . .

I wipe the smeared window with my left hand, my wedding ring tapping on the glass. I notice how chapped and swollen my fingers are these days, how the flesh bulges tight and shiny below my knuckle. There was a time when this thin band of gold would slip off. Now getting it off will not be easy. It doesn't budge as I try to twist it between the thumb and index finger of my right hand. It would have been our fiftieth wedding anniversary this June. Congratulations would have been in order. *Llongyfarchiadau!*

That's the thing about arranged marriages. Made to last. The deal was sealed at Carmarthen Mart. Father had been there with the cattle when I was sold off with the nod of the head and a gnarled handshake along with half a dozen Welsh Blacks and a *coffer bach** to a Mr. Matthias Beynon, Farmer, Llangennith. A tidy sort, he'd said, not a Welsh speaker and not chapel either; but a good man, he was sure, with a fair few acres. I later learned he didn't even have his own lorry, let alone a car. He'd come to Carmarthen with G.I. Thomas, Llanrhidian who did haulage. He relied on them to get about. He always relied on someone.

The farmer wants a wife
The farmer wants a wife
E-I-E-I-O the farmer wants a wife

But I went willingly. There was no sign of the shiny ring through my nostrils like a bull as he led me to Well Park Farm.

. . . Gowerton . . . Dunvant . . . Upper Killay . . .

They're staring at me, these early-morning commuters. Do I look different? Or just like any other seventy-year-old recently-widowed woman on a bus with a shopping bag on her lap? Different. *Gwahanol.* It sounds so much gentler in Welsh, airy and breathy in the mouth. Things would have been different, I suppose, if there'd been children. *The farm needs children, Gwen,* he'd say, *sons. It's the way things are on the land.*

> *The wife wants a child*
> *The wife wants a child*
> *E-I-E-I-O the wife wants a child*

I watch and listen as a young couple up front giggle and *cwtsh* up to each other. She's whispering so close to his ear. I wonder if she's cooing the love-words I once longed to use but never had the chance to give an airing. How I would have loved the feel of uttering *cariad*, rolling its long Welsh vowels around my mouth's empty chamber.

For almost fifty years I've seen rams put to the ewe, bulls mounting cows from the kitchen window, making the beast with two backs. I've pulled lambs wet and slimy, watched their mothers lick them clean, suckle them from swollen teats. I've sat in the sheds long into the night, waiting for the cows to calve, listened to the primeval groan of their labour as nature took over.

He never actually said it, but I could see it etched on his face, read it in the stoop of his shoulders, the set of his jaw: *Your father sold me a dud, a barren bitch. Thought you would have been good breeding stock.* Until one day he simply stated: *We'd better just sleep back to back from now on, Gwen.*

Alone. *Ar ben fy hun.*

Yet we were always together; yoked. We never actually seemed to go anywhere, no weekends off, no holidays, constantly tethered to the land. But surely we must have gone somewhere? To the next village perhaps, or to search for lost stock that had roamed across the common up to the top of the Down. We'd go on the red Ferguson: him cupped in the metal seat and me planted behind him, legs astride, my hands placed on his shoulders for support.

Apart from that, we'd be pressed in the kitchen: me at the sink looking out over the meadow, on to the sea beyond, and him hunched over his tea, slurping through his toothless gums, waiting for it to stop raining, always waiting for the front to pass through.

And when there was a break in the clouds, he'd rise from the table, scrape the chair across the flags, don his flat cap and green wellies, pick up his stick, slam the front door behind him, and be gone without a word.

There was a crooked man, and he walked a crooked mile
He found a crooked sixpence upon a crooked stile
He bought a crooked cat which caught a crooked mouse
And they all lived together in a little crooked house
. . . Killay . . . Sketty . . . Uplands

Almost there now. I know this journey like the back of my rough hand. Five more minutes and we'll draw into the bus station and I'll alight, my shopping back at the ready, and head for the market. Just a five-minute stroll. Though I have nothing to buy this morning, nothing to fetch and carry, nothing to take back and put in front of him, one o'clock sharp when he likes his dinner. I do not have to be at the ready, standing there at the side of the table, a hired hand, slicing bread, pouring tea, waiting until he's had everything he wants before eventually taking my place.

Nothing. *Dim.*

As I get off the bus, the cold hits me. Damp cold. Grey, Swansea cold. And a wind off the bay that seems to wheeze through the concourse, making it hard to catch my breath. I am glad of the warmth of the market and the momentary comfort. I am pulled, as ever, to the open stalls at the far end;

the wooden tables piled high with caulies, potatoes, strange-shaped carrots. And then on, to the cockles and the laver bread: *What can I do for you today, Mrs. Beynon? Usual, is it?*

Usual? *Run peth ag arfer?*

Dim, diolch. Nothing, thanks.

I can't tell them that today is not usual and that I have no appetite at all, just a gnawing feeling that feels like hunger, but is deeper. It is all too much, too busy: the shoppers jostling me with their plastic carrier bags, the stale odour of cigarettes hanging on their coats, the smell of cooking and grease – faggots, pies, chips. And the noise, there is an incessant high-pitched hum in my head as though the world is out of tune. I need to go, get home.

I retrace my steps, my empty bag lolling on my arm. I find a seat in the bus station and watch the litter dance on the blast of cold air that is slicing at my swollen ankles and wait for the next bus. I've no idea of the time, but there's no rush. Not even a need to go home.

I take out my bus pass and see the possibility of endless travel on Welsh roads, for free, courtesy of the Welsh Government.

Free. *Am ddim.*

I could go anywhere. Everywhere is new and fresh, bursting with possibility when you have never been anywhere. I could go back to Llandowror, the old farm; though there's no one at home there anymore. Dead. *Wedi marw.* Nor anyone in Llangennith. All gone and me still here. For the first time in my life I feel I have freedom and choices, my get-out-of-jail pass clutched in my hand. And yet I am rooted to a bench in a bus station that I've come to for half a century.

I show my pass to the familiar, smiling-faced Nepalese

driver on the 116 back to Llangennith. *That was quick, Mrs. Beynon*, he says. *Nothing you fancied, today?* I don't feel like talking, just clutch my bag close to me and sink into the usual seat for the journey home.

Swansea . . . Uplands . . . Sketty . . . Killay . . . Upper Killay . . . Gowerton . . .

Now the landscape is loosening and with it the tightness in my chest. I'm on the right, still three rows from the front, the estuary now in full flood, transforming the drabness of the vast expanse of dull mud and concealing the pills gouged in the sand. Apart from me and the driver, the bus is empty. After all it's still only mid-morning and who apart from me would be travelling to the western edge of the peninsula on a winter's day? I feel lulled by the engine and the warmth of the heating. Calmer. Stiller.

. . . Penclawdd . . . Crofty . . . Llanmorlais . . . Llanrhidian . . .

We are going back to Llangennith 'the quick way' via Oldwalls and Burry Green. And sooner than I'd anticipated, the ocean's in view. We rumble down the hill into the village and the bus slows to drop me off at the farm before the bend. *Drive on*, I say, *down into the village to the end of the road*. He doesn't say anything, but I catch his eyes meeting mine in his rear-view mirror.

It's a no-through road where the bus terminates and turns. I thank the driver very much and wish him a good day as he opens the automatic doors for me to get off. The wind is strong in my face; on my lips, the taste of salt. My limbs are pulling me in a new direction, so I don't turn and walk back up the hill towards the farm, but on, along the single-file track that leads towards the beach at Broughton, facing north-west across the estuary to Carmarthenshire.

My empty shopping bag is light and purposeless on my left arm, so I cast it into the wind and watch it come to rest in the hedgerow. My brown leather handbag weighs heavier on my right arm which is beginning to ache. I unclasp it and hear my mother's words echo down the years: Who was I? *Pwy oeddwn i?* Who am I, *Pwy ydw i?* I unburden myself of the contents, tipping them purposefully into the desiccated bracken as I walk down the lane. My load lighter now, I feel unencumbered, feathery.

I am left with just the bus pass in my hand. I focus on the passport-size image of myself staring back at me, serious, distant. It disturbs me. I can't make out if *she's* anything like *me* anymore, Mrs. G. Beynon.

I walk on, a new and impulsive energy surging through me. With a grand flourish, I hurl my bus pass into the brittle nettles and the spite of bare blackthorn. I have no further use for it. My pace quickens, my heart pounds quickly as I approach the end of the tarmac lane and pick up the unmade track across the fields that fall off to the sea. *Gwen, ydw i a dwi'n mynd i deithio*. I'm Gwen and I'm going travelling. I say it out loud it in my mother tongue, the sensation stimulating my taste buds.

Mynd drot drot ar y gaseg wen
Mynd drot drot i'r dre
Mam yn dod 'nôl dros fryn a dôl
A rhywbeth neis neis i de*

LOOK WHAT THE WIND'S BLOWN IN

H E A R R I V E S W I T H the first cold day of autumn. Through the conservatory window I see him in the front seat of the 4x4. He looks lost in the cavernous space, shrunken, like a child again, strapped tight in the seat belt. I wave, but he doesn't wave back, nor does he smile. His eyes seem fixed on something that only he can see. They look even darker than I remember, a look I've only ever seen in the eyes of hungry children in television campaigns.

My husband opens the passenger door for him and supports him as he climbs down. A blizzard of brown leaves swirls around his ankles as he tries to get his balance on the drive. I have the feeling that he could be swept away on the next gust. He picks his way towards the door, with the aid of his gnarled walking stick, too short for him, so that his meagre frame is bent to forty-five degrees to accommodate it. The fabric of his fawn trousers looks too thin for this weather: there's a show of sock between hem and shoe and the material flaps wildly in the wind, as though there's nothing beneath for it to cling to.

"Look what the wind's blown in," my husband says as he ushers his father inside.

"Shush," I say, turning to Jack. "Don't take any notice of him. Come and have a sit down."

As I kiss him on the cheek, there's an unfamiliar odour. I

watch him make for the chair in the corner of the room, next to the window, watch him as he collapses back into its arms, places his stick beside him as if marking out his territory.

"I don't want to be here," he says. "I told *him* I didn't want to come."

"I know that, Jack. But look at you. What on earth have you been doing to yourself?"

"He can't be bothered to eat. That's what he's been doing to himself," says my husband.

"Shut up, Alan," I say, "he's ill. Look at him."

"That's right, girl," he says. "Ill I am. From the feet up."

"Look, let's not argue," I say, "just stay till we get you back on your feet again. Get you checked out. Get some meat on you so you can get back to Francis Street."

Later, we sit down to eat together at the table. He troughs his minced beef with a fork in his right hand, head down, not a word uttered between mouthfuls.

"Hungry, Jack?" I say. "You've almost taken the pattern off the plate."

"Needed a good feed," he says. "No-one to cook for me now."

"There's you," says my husband to him. "You can't expect to live on digestive biscuits."

"Women's work," Jack says and pushes his plate to the middle of the table, gets up and takes up what looks like is going to be his place, in the chair he'd sat in earlier. He bangs his stick on the floor and turns his head to look out of the window.

After we've got him upstairs to bed, my husband and I sit on the settee opposite the empty chair, where the stick remains, propped against the wall, the blue leather case for his reading glasses on the arm, a tissue packet alongside.

"You don't know what you've let yourself in for," my husband says, "you don't know what he's like."

"He's not well. Needs looking after. Needs to see a doctor," I say.

"You'll never change his ways," he goes on.

"A bit of support for the time being and then sheltered housing or something."

"Needs shooting, if you ask me."

And then he gets up and goes to bed.

Over breakfast the next day, I notice brown crusted scabs above the neckline of Jack's vest, which he wears under the blue shirt he arrived in the day before. The vest is yellowed, the rim soiled brown. And that odour is still strong.

"They look cancerous," I whisper to my husband in the kitchen. "Take him over to the surgery."

"He's filthy. I can't take him over like that."

"He can't look after himself. Look how frail he is. Gone eighty, for God's sake."

"Frail be buggered. He's a dirty, lazy sod. Don't be fooled by age," he says. "Needs hosing down."

"Give him some respect. He's your father."

"So? Why d'you think my mother threw him out?"

All of a sudden I realise that I don't know anything about my husband really. His past. His relationship with his mother. His father. I feel like a sticking plaster that just might not hold the wound, heal the split. But I'll give it a go.

"Alan's going to take you to the doctor, Jack," I say. "See what's making you so poorly. OK with you?"

"Aye. Doctors up Merthyr don't know what they're doing.

Said there's nothing wrong . . . *just* the arthritis. Told 'em I'm dying from the feet up."

"What d'you mean by that?"

"Sick, girl. That's what I am. Sick. Something serious going on that they're too stupid to find. Doctors down by 'ere will find it. Mark my words."

"D'you mean those spots?"

"No, not the spots. Something inside. And nerves."

"But what are those?" I ask, pointing to the crusty scabs.

"Put a bit of talc on them, I have. Shower's packed up."

"How long?"

"Can't remember. Ages."

"Why haven't you got it fixed? Had someone in? We could have sorted it for you."

"Don't like strangers in the house. Anyway, managed with a swill."

"Well, you can have a nice shower now before Alan takes you over to the doctor. And then we can talk about Francis Street. Perhaps it's getting a bit too much for you to manage?"

"It's like a palace, girl. Beautiful," he says.

He's weak on his feet as Alan and I walk him to the downstairs wet room. I watch as offspring becomes parent as Alan unbuttons Jack's blue shirt and tosses it into the laundry room. Jack raises his arms in the air as Alan lifts his vest up over his head, and off, dropping it to the floor. I heave silently at his naked torso: ribs exposed, chest concave, and the encrusted spots are there, all over. It is more serious than I had imagined.

He doesn't flinch that I'm present as Alan continues to undress him, taking down his trousers to reveal his muscle-wasted legs. And finally, his underpants. For some reason that

Jack cannot explain, there are two pairs, a dark navy boxer pair with filthy Y-fronts underneath. Jack leans against the washbowl as Alan uses the hand-held shower. I watch as he flannels his face and sponges his naked back and buttocks. I have the urge to cry; but Alan is unmoved, rubbing harder and harder to get him clean. He is filthy. Months, perhaps years, of oil and dirt layered on his skin. The crusts come off on the flannel.

Alan finds spare pants – two pairs – socks, a vest, a blue shirt and chinos, and dresses him firmly, rolling the trouser legs up and the sleeves of the shirt. Though the clothes don't fit properly, they make him look different somehow. It's not just that they're clean. It's something about the fabric, the quality of the shirt, the colour perhaps. They're nothing like he has ever had on his back in his whole eighty years.

"There," I say, "good as new."

"Don't think so, girl. Your doctors down here will prove me right."

⚓

On his return, he enters the room like a storm. No need for my husband's support, or the stick which he points at the chair in the corner before he charges across the room. His temper seems to be giving him some inner strength, his eyes are angry, his jaw set with some kind of boiling agenda. He sits down with a flourish and draws one of our woven Welsh *Melin Tregwynt** blankets over his lap. He places his bony hands on top and sighs loudly.

"Well? How d'you get on over there? What did they say?" I ask.

Before he has chance to answer, if perhaps he ever would have, Alan comes in and throws the car keys on to the table.

"Like I said. Nothing wrong with him. Malnourished. Weak as a kitten," he says.

"Well, that's good news, then," I say.

"Clean bill of health, Dad," Alan shouts over at his father. "It's official. Straight from the medic's mouth."

"Rubbish," says Jack. "Just as bad these Gower doctors as those up Merthyr. Cocodomol they've given me. Cocodomol."

And he rattles the mild pain killers like maracas before banging the container down on the windowsill.

"You'll see how ill I am. The lot of you. Just you wait and see," he says.

"You've got to eat, Jack," I say, "that's why you're weak. It's like putting petrol in the car. It's not that hard."

"Not my job to cook for myself. He's got you!"

I try to ignore the politics of this and for the first time can see what my husband has been going on about. Keep calm. Be conciliatory. Try another tactic.

"You don't even have to cook. Just have good food – cheese, fruit, cold meats. What about meals on wheels?"

"They're not coming in my house. Thieves, they are."

"What about a flat then? Say in a sheltered block. Can keep yourself to yourself. Have your own place, your own front door, your own key. But there'll be someone there if you need them. You can have your very own buzzer. And you can have your meals done. And company might be nice," I try.

"Don't need company. Got the radio. That's all the company I need."

"Just have a look at one of these sheltered places, Jack. You never know, you might like it. You can't go back to Francis

Street – the place is falling down over your head, caving in."

"I'll see, girl. Just let me alone for the time being. I'll see."

❧

As the weeks pass, he gets fatter; fitter, more demanding. Now he's picky about what I place in front of him, telling me forcibly what food he likes, what I prepare that he thinks is *quite disgusting*.

"It's only mince, Jack," I cajole, "you like that. Easy to chew. To digest."

"There's muck on it. Spicy. Stomach can't stand it," he says.

"It's just the same as you had the first day you got here," I argue.

"Tastes different to me, girl. Horrible."

My husband begins to smirk. Says nothing, but a smile starts to appear on his face which says, *I told you so*. Jack says nothing too, but eases into his throne in the corner, his blanket pulled over him, his hand firmly over the handle of the stick which he taps, taps, taps on the slate floor, the radio tuned in to his favourite programme. Alan and I sit in silence on the settee opposite him, strangers in our own home. Jack goes to bed later and later. We take to our beds earlier and earlier. Sometimes Jack does not go to bed at all; instead sits bolt upright in the chair till morning comes and another day begins.

"You know what the cussed sod wants, don't you?" Alan whispers to me upstairs.

I ask him why we both feel the need to whisper in our own home. And no, I don't know what Jack wants or what I can do about it.

"You. You to look after him. Here."

"But I have to work. I can't."

"He's taking over, like I said he would. Imposing himself on us."

"Is that what he thinks I'm for? To look after him? I mean, there's nothing really wrong with him."

"You're a woman, aren't you?"

"God, Alan. He'll have to go."

⚘

The following morning, he's there in the chair, waiting for his breakfast to be put on the table.

"Wondering when you'd be down, girl," he says. "Sitting here starving, I am."

"You know where the fridge is, Jack. You're not disabled, you know. Quite capable of getting yourself some cereal, a cup of tea."

"Rather you did it. Not well today."

"Well, I'd rather not," I say. "You need to learn to do it yourself. For your own good."

"At my age?" he says and strides to the table.

"About time we had a look at a sheltered place, I think. Best for us all."

"I'll have a look," he agrees, "but I'm not promising, mind."

⚘

Jack and I drive to Merthyr. There's a flat in sheltered accommodation at Bodalaw* right opposite the doctors' surgery and near to the town centre. Jack tells me in the car that he knows a couple of blokes in there, used to work with him in the Hoover factory before it closed down. Not that he likes them, mind. Just because they're old like him, he doesn't have to like them. The flat is light and freshly painted with brand-spanking-new appliances in the kitchen.

"All you'll have to do is hang your clothes in the wardrobe; I'll get everything new for you: bedding, curtains, settee. A fresh start. Nothing at all to worry about. It'll take me a couple of days to buy the stuff and furnish it and then you can move in," I say.

"Fit for a king," he says. "Thank you, girl, thank you very much."

I take him back to Gower for a little while longer. I shop for a single bed that'll be easy for him to get in and out of, a sofa which I make sure has a high back for his neck, a recliner chair with a footstool, a new TV with a remote, matching curtains and cushions, electric kettle, a tea pot, white crockery and full set of stainless steel cutlery. I furnish it with care as if I was doing it for myself, as if it were my very own new home. I place pot pourri in the bathroom, scented candles on the sideboard, and a large bunch of white lilies in a glass vase on the window sill. I pride myself on finding this place. Making it happen. Sorting it. It gives me a good feeling that I've done this for him. He could be safe and happy here. And I'll feel a lot better.

This time it's Alan who stands in the conservatory and waves his father and me off in the 4x4. I'm taking him back to Francis Street. There are a few bits he wants to sort out: sentimental photographs off the mantelpiece, some of his favourite books and CDs. He has money in brown envelopes that he's tucked in drawers and between magazines – he needs to get it all together before he leaves. He wants to say his goodbyes to Mrs. Williams next door. She's been very kind to him over the years, after all. Done his shopping, puts the Hoover over now and again, brings him the newspaper, keeps an eye of him. He wants to say fond farewells to the old place too, lots of memories there, he says. Needs a bit of time on his own.

I watch him turn his key in the front door and step inside. Empty milk bottles are gathered in the porch and I wonder why he has never put them out on the doorstep. There are scores of pairs of shoes stacked in the living room, lined up under the sideboard as if he needs all these shoes for the places he might go, though never goes anywhere anymore. In the kitchen there is packet after packet of digestive biscuits and stacks of old newspapers and kitchen roll folded in squares. Everywhere there is paper. A layer of dust coats the sideboard where there are framed pictures, women mostly – his mother, his sister, his ex – all dead and gone now. There's one of me too with Alan when we got married.

"Sure you'll be alright here on your own? Only a short while now," I say.

"Right as rain," he says. "You get back to Alan now. He'll be waiting for his dinner."

"I'll give you a ring later. Let you know I'm home. See if you're OK."

"No need. But if it makes you feel better," he says.

I kiss him on the cheek. There's a new, clean smell of Dove. My soap.

As promised, when I get back I dial his number. I let it ring and ring but he doesn't answer. I leave a message, asking him to just pick up the phone and tell me he's alright. But he doesn't ring back.

"D'you think he's okay?" I ask Alan.

"Course he is. Just doesn't want to pick up the phone, that's all."

"Why not?"

"Why d'you think?"

"I don't know, I mean it isn't as if I'm making big demands on him. It'll only take a second. Put my mind at rest."

"I'm ringing him again. I'll keep on till he picks up."

"You're wasting your time, you know. He won't budge."

For two days, I ring and leave messages, but he doesn't get back to me. I decide to go up.

"Come with me, Alan. He's your father. I'm worried. I want to know when he's going to move in to Bodalaw. They keep asking me."

"I'm not coming. I'm done with it," he says.

꧁

It's raining and dark as I drive along the A465 Heads of the Valley Road. It always seems to be raining up here. I turn off through the Pant Estate and down into Francis Street. They all look the same to me these terraces, drab, grey, closing in on each other. I pull up outside number 11, the shabbiest in a shabby row, and get out of the car. I ring the bell and wait for him to come to the door. No-one comes. Perhaps he's afraid of intruders, I think. I'll ring on the mobile and tell him I'm outside in the rain, just to make him feel safer. Still, he doesn't pick up. The front curtains are drawn but the light is on inside. I rap on the glass and shout: *Jack. It's me, Susan. Let me in.* I keep rapping, a frenzied rapping until my knuckles are sore. Through the gap in the curtains, I see him. He's in his leatherette chair with the winged back, a cushion behind his neck. He's staring out in front of him yet I can't hear the sound of a radio or see the white light and flickering glare of the television. His tartan rug is draped over his legs, his stick leaning against his nest of tables. On the surface is his reading lamp, his blue glasses case, a packet of digestive biscuits and a heap of used and crinkled tissues. For a brief second, he turns his head towards the sound at the window and those deep brown eyes of his meet mine. They have that look in them again. And then he turns back to focus on whatever it is was he was looking at before, pressing his hands down hard onto the arms of his chair.

THE GREY MARE

WHETHER IT WAS the heat, or all the beer he'd drunk after finally managing to get the hay in on his own that August night, but Brinley Taylor could only sleep in fits. He'd had that dream again, the same one that had recurred for almost five years. He'd had his brother by the throat, throttling him slowly, enjoying the terror in his eyes. He'd squeezed and squeezed with his thumbs on his airways until the breath had left him and his body had gone limp in his hands. When Brinley had woken, his forehead was beaded with sweat. His torso was tense and rigid and he felt as though the air in the bedroom had weight, pressing down heavy on his chest, taking his own breath away.

The dream had unsettled him this time more than ever: so much so that he couldn't contemplate turning over and trying to get back to sleep. Instead, he got out of bed, walked along the corridor into the kitchen, keyed in the code to the safe in the pantry, took out the key and unlocked the tall cupboard in the corner. Minutes later, he found himself across the stock fence that separated his bungalow standing on fifty acres from his brother's farm with its two hundred and fifty acres of prime agricultural land. Once it had been just one farm of three hundred acres. It was still known to the Gower locals and the postman simply as The Taylors, Muzzard Farm.

He walked with urgency. There were things that needed doing. The rough grass was springy under his boots and seemed to lift him along. He found his pace quickening as he drew nearer to the meadow. With every step, a new emotion flooded his head. There was self-pity, yes he'd own up to that. But self-doubt, no. Mostly there was a festering anger. What had he ever done to deserve his mother to say he'd been an *afterthought*? He'd never asked to hear her say that he hadn't been planned, that he'd been *born on the change* twenty years after his brother, Lyndon. He'd never asked to be written out of the farm in the will. They could have run it together, Lyndon and him, couldn't they? *Can't let you have more than fifty acres*, the bastard had said, *fifty more than Mother'd have given you*. How the hell could he live off that? Bloody impossible. He was his brother, for God's sake. But Lyndon had only said that he had a family now, needed to think about the future, had to pass something on.

That's when the fence had gone up along with the little bungalow and Brinley started to scratch a living: ewes which lambed in spring which he sold for a pittance, ewes which weren't worth shearing anymore as there was nothing in fleeces, twenty or so heifers which gave him a bit more but not enough to stop him having to get work in the local abattoir to make ends meet. He had no idea what his future would hold.

He'd never forget the taste of ozone in the air that night as he ploughed across his brother's land. The thunder would come later. He wouldn't forget the look in the grey mare's eyes either as he approached her through the lower meadow, the clover grass wet against his pyjama bottoms. The dark brown eyes had a stoic acceptance about them, full with milky liquid. She wasn't spooked at all: didn't pace or hoof, move any of those fine fetlocks of hers, or let out a snort. Her ears pricked just ever so slightly as he drew nearer, and said, *sorry girl*, before he cocked the shotgun and blasted her brains out.

Brinley watched the great mass of mare heave to the ground with a finality that shocked him. He'd never thought himself capable of such an act of violence. If someone had told him all those years ago that he'd kill his young niece's best show pony, deny her the pleasure of cantering around those jumps that her father had erected for her, he wouldn't have thought it possible. But he'd done it. He could smell the spent cartridge; the lifeless hulk on its side on the grass.

His legs started to shake and he sank to the ground alongside the mare to try and hold himself together. From his perspective, it was as though she was sleeping and he expected her to stir at any second, or to see her bulking abdomen rise and fall. But she was as still as only death can be. Brinley felt a peace that came from her, a fleeting nothingness that he hadn't felt in years.

He'd found it easy to get back to sleep after that, bloated with the smug satisfaction that his brother wouldn't be feeling so calm when he rose in the morning and found the prize mare slaughtered in the meadow. Brinley felt bad about his niece, she didn't really deserve to feel the pain and the grief that she'd feel; but sometimes kids had to suffer things they didn't ask for.

Brinley wondered whether his brother would know it was him who'd shot the mare. There'd be big consequences, if he did. There'd be the sobs of the little girl and a story Lyndon would have to tell her of some wicked person who'd come in the night under the din of the thunder to carry out this deed and yes, it was sad, that there were such people in this world. There'd be the palaver of dealing with the fallen mare: whether Lyndon would decide to dig a pit and incinerate himself as he could legally, or have the Ministry come and take the carcass away. Lyndon wasn't one, like some in these parts, who'd leave an animal rot somewhere quiet. Brinley would wait for the consequences, hand himself over willingly to their inevitability. It would be a release he thought, like vomiting, when you had felt sick for too long.

Days passed. Summer became autumn became winter. Life at the farm split by blood went on as it had done for the past five years: there was no seething visit to the bungalow, no vitriolic accusations that were itching to be answered. Nothing. Not a word. Brinley found it hard to believe that Lyndon had not automatically assumed it was him: if the situation had been reversed, he would have known with a brother's intuition deep in the gut. They shared the same DNA for God's sake, had shared their mother's womb at different times in her life, suckled at the same breasts. Brinley knew then that there was nothing as dead as dead love.

The guilt Brinley had felt in the first few months after the event curdled in his stomach but he was surprised that it eased with time. When August came around again, he sometimes wondered whether it had ever happened at all. Life on the other side of the fence had moved on, his little niece was smiling again with a new pony to replace the one that had gone in the night. Things could quickly be forgotten, by everyone, it seemed.

August brought a woman into Brinley's life too. He'd been in school with her, but hadn't had any inclinations towards her until he saw Mary Grove again at a Young Farmer's pig roast at Weobley Castle. She wasn't exactly what you'd call a looker, but she'd make a great farmer's wife judging by the build on her. She was the only child at Tankey Lake Farm, Llangennith: she'd been bred for the job and she'd be good to breed too: heavy-hipped and strong. She'd be the making of him. He'd be a proper farmer one day too, all those acres that would come with her on their marriage. He would have land, kids of his own, something he could pass on, just like fucking Lyndon.

Brinley knew how people all over Gower talked about what went on at Muzzard between the two brothers and what didn't. They made up stories to fill the gaps. He wondered if anything had ever come out about the dead mare. Wondered if Mary had heard anything. If she had, she never said. But the thought that it might come out picked at Brinley constantly.

"How about we get married?" he said to Mary.

"What's the rush?" she said. "Do I seem that desperate?"

"No, but . . . kids?"

"Next summer, then. Give us time to plan."

"Sooner. How about a winter wedding? New Year's Day? A fresh page in our lives?"

"You'll make a lovely, dad, you know."

"D'you think so?" Brinley said.

And so it was decided.

⁂

Just when things seemed to be going well for the first time in his life, that autumn as Mary and her family busied themselves with the minutiae of planning a village wedding for an only girl, Brinley's dreams started to invade his sleep again. They weren't of his brother this time, but of the grey mare. Every night he'd kill that mare. Over and over again, he'd kill her in exactly the same calculating way. In the dream she'd be alive in the meadow, her mane tossed back, hooves thundering as she cantered around the perimeter of the field as she saw him draw near. *Quiet girl, it's alright,* he'd say. But the horse sensed the fear in the air, flared her nostrils at its distinctive stench. And then Brinley would see those eyes, those knowing eyes full of foreboding as she knew her end was near. And then he'd splatter her bloody brains out again and again and again.

He would wake with a start from the dream at the sound of the shotgun and he would sit bolt upright in his bed, sweating and shaking just as he'd done on the night it had happened. For this dream told him, repeatedly, that it had all actually happened.

There were never any scenes in the dream of his brother: he found that strange, that the consequences didn't play out. All he saw was that damn mare. He saw it where he had left it in the wet meadow, swelling and distorting, the belly distending. Saw crows and magpies perched on its back, beaking and bobbing its drying hide, pecking into the meat below. Saw buzzards gorging on the carrion. Watched the flies taking hold of the flesh, the maggots crawl and feast. Saw the beast picked clean until only a dried heap of bones remained and a skull with the eyes gouged and the sockets hollow and exposed.

It was hard to shake off the feeling he was left with as daylight broke. He tried to work it off, told Mary his subdued mood was due to the wedding. Jitters. And no, he wasn't changing his mind. He couldn't wait.

꧁

The Groves wanted to put on a good show for their only daughter. It would be a big wedding. They'd do it in the Gower way. The gates of the church at St Cenydd's would be tied with ribbon until the happy couple gave money to be let out after the ceremony; the local farmers would be standing outside with their guns and would fire into the air as a salute to the married couple as they emerged from the churchyard and onto the village green. It would be a wedding, the scale of which people would talk about for years to come. Brinley would have his stag do and Mary her hen do; but the Groves insisted that it wouldn't be the night before the wedding. That wasn't the way things were done in these parts.

On New Year's Eve it was open house at Tankey Lake Farm: everyone in the village who was coming to the wedding or not was welcome to come for a drink, and toast the happy couple. The Groves had got barrels of beer from The King's Head, and there was seasonal mulled wine simmering on the range, the scent of cinnamon in the air. All the wedding presents were on show in the sitting room: towels and toasters, cut glass vases and wine goblets and tumblers, cutlery sets and candelabra, an electric carving knife and a deep-fat fryer. Everything one could ever wish for. Inside the Christmas tree remained tastefully decorated and lit with white lights and the white light theme had been extended outside too: the porch was twinkling with tiny fairy-lights like stars which lit up the yard along with the moon, just on the wane.

By 10 p.m. the farmhouse was heaving, the drink flowing and there was much tale-telling of goings-on in Gower. But of Muzzard there was not a whisper. People came and went:

there was no set time to come or go. It would finish up when it did. Some planned to stay to see the New Year in with a song. Edna Grove got on the piano and accompanied Stan Grove as he kicked things off with 'Because', an old favourite from their youth. A group of farmers stood up and together did the 'Bold Gendarmes' from Gilbert and Sullivan. When the doorbell went, as was the custom, the bride-to-be and her groom would go to the door to receive the guests and bring them in.

It must have been about 11.45 p.m. that Brinley remembers the singing had become slightly maudlin. It always did with the drink. Soon there were hymns, and then hymns in Welsh and the television was on in the corner with the sound turned down but ready for Big Ben to strike the New Year in. And then he heard the doorbell go.

"They're cutting it fine," he said to Mary. "Just in time."

Hand in hand, they left the noise of the sitting room, shut the door behind them and walked along the passage to the front porch. As Brinley opened the front door, it was the brilliance of the white that hit him, ghostly white under the fairy lights and the winter moon. He'd know those eyes anywhere; though of course there were no eyes now, just the sockets in the immense cathedral of a skull which was in close-up, inches from his face. Below the skull was a white cotton sheet, draped loosely over a figure it completely obscured. The cotton rose and fell just slightly in the cold breeze to reveal the feet which now stood on the step. He clutched Mary's hand tightly as the voice within the skull began to sing an old wassailing song, pleading for admittance and to be the entertainment to bring in the New Year. He'd know that voice anywhere.

THE SANDS ARE SINGING

S ARAH HAS STARTED cleaning the caravan from top to bottom. Even though it is August Bank Holiday Monday, it has to be done. Everything must be pulled out, washed, wiped, sprayed, polished and put back in its exact place, just so: leather-bound books, Dickens, Bronte, a bible. She runs her fingers across the silver-framed photograph on the shelf, after she's buffed it till it gleams. She wonders what her five-year-old boy would look like now. She can't imagine him as a man, still expects him to come bounding in through the door at any moment.

She turns at the tap on the window. She knows her brother will come to see if she's alright today.

"Not cleaning on a day like this, are we?" Richard shouts through the half-opened window. He has walked across the small field that separates his cottage from her caravan. He likes to keep an eye on his sister the way he has done for over forty-five years, ever since he sited the old caravan on his small holding for her and Evan.

"Don't start now, Richard. You know what I'm like," she replies.

"Looks like you're expecting visitors for a change. Been going at it hell for leather."

She doesn't answer but carries on dusting the surfaces, plumping the cushions.

"Don't need to ask if you're going on your walk, then?"

"What do you think?"

Soon after, her arthritic hands struggle to turn the key in the rusty, salt-encrusted lock of the door and she stands outside and allows herself to take stock for a moment. The view from the top of Welsh Moor out over the estuary is breath-taking on a day like this: big skies, floating cumulus, just the merest hint of a breeze. You just wouldn't know how quickly things could change out there. There's a feeling of the season's ending about: the swallows lining up on the wires, things in transition, a certain poignancy in the sunshine that she knows will not last.

With the chrysanthemums wrapped in cellophane tucked under her arm and her well-worn shopping bag, she sets out along the single-file track. It's not so bad going down; the momentum propelling her ageing body, her swollen legs. She is already anticipating the return slog: the steep gradient, the gasps of breath. How long things can go on like this she doesn't know; but do it, she must.

Hardly a car ever passes along this narrow lane: weeds are pushing up like memories through the cracks in the tarmac and small stones litter the surface. She takes care to avoid them. Like people. Though not a soul passes her on this journey: no one she has to raise her head and smile at, no one she feels obliged to say *Good morning* to.

As she rounds the last bend, the sight of the ruined chapel at Hermon comes into view. There at the side of the lane it stands: forlorn, overgrown with bramble and ivy, the once proud building a hollow shell, roofless apart from the wooden trusses which let the sky in. The arched windows are without glass, the render dulled and peeling, revealing patches of grey-brown stone here and there. Inside the ruined space the walls are daubed red with fresh graffiti fired from aerosol cans – grotesque faces and slogans – *Fuck God* – and crisp packets, empty cans of Strongbow cider and fragments of broken headstones which are strewn among the hip-high grass that now carpets this hallowed space. She lowers her head to read: *Thy will be done.*

In her mind she can see herself as a teenager again in the chapel, see its pews thronged with people, hear the hymns of Sundays past. And she sees him, Eldon, the young minister at the pulpit, thumping out his sermon with a deep passion in his pained voice. How she'd loved to listen to him speaking: not so much for what he'd said, but the way he'd said things. His convictions. He was the sort of man who could make her believe in things too, if she'd allow herself.

The chapel had been painted white then, still shining out like a beacon to those who had once navigated the difficult waters of the Burry Estuary below. And perhaps life itself. But now there is something unruly and heathen again here, she thinks, spreading out of control like bindweed.

There's no one visiting the graveyard this holiday morning apart from her. She feels at home in the solitariness of it. She walks up and down between the rows of graves: the ornate black marbled ones with the gold lettering . . .

To live in the hearts of those that live
Is not to die

. . . the lichen covered grey-green stones with the indecipherable inscriptions. The tiny, raw-earthed mound pillowed with white blooms and fresh messages of sympathy on white cards. No name there to mark this short life as yet; but there will be. She longs for a patch of earth for her Evan just like this: somewhere to come and acknowledge that he once lived, somewhere to place the flowers that she is carrying that she will scatter later anonymously on the garden of remembrance in the top of the yard.

She heaves her body up the grassy slope where she sits on the bench in the corner of the cemetery, sheltered by the trees and the wall of the crumbling chapel. The rooks circle ahead cawing in a language she wishes she understood. From here she gazes out across the estuary, watching the low clouds smudging the horizon, listening for the familiar sound of the gulls. She can see a Land Rover and trailer far out at the lip of the Loughor, the stooped silhouettes of the pickers: they're mostly men these days. Her back aches with the looking. She reaches into her bag and lifts out her Thermos flask and small Tupperware container, pours herself some hot and sweet milky tea into the plastic mug, takes a small sandwich and sits, drifting into deep thought, her eyes peeled on the sands in the distance.

And then as though from nowhere, there's a young woman joining her on the same small bench, a young woman with fair hair scraped back off her bony face, wearing jeans and train- ers. The young woman does not say *Good morning* and Sarah isn't sure whether this is a good or a bad thing. *Youth*, she thinks and goes on eating her sandwich wishing the intruder was not there with her in her space. She wishes the bench was bigger. For even though the clothes are different, there is something in this young woman that reminds Sarah of the girl she once was.

The silent young woman delves into her plastic Tesco carrier bag and brings out a can of Coke, pulls back the ring and begins to swig. She rifles through the bag a second time and then has a small leather pouch on her lap and she's taking strands of tobacco and placing them hurriedly along a Rizla paper, rolling up the filled cylinder in her shaking hands and sealing the edge of the fine paper with a long lick of her tongue. She proceeds to light-up, striking a match and cupping the flame in her hand, fearful of it going out. The smell of phosphorous fills the space between them. It's a smell Sarah has not smelled for longer than she cares to remember.

"Sorry," the girl says, "didn't ask if you'd mind. World of my own."

"That's alright. Doesn't bother me. Used to smoke myself. Long time ago now, mind," says Sarah.

She forgets sometimes that she was young: seems to have been old for most of her life. Forgets that a chapel-going girl like her used to like a cigarette. Not in the house at Station Road. Just when she was out. Being *chapel* as they put it, her parents didn't smoke. Didn't drink. Didn't gamble. They didn't seem to do anything much to do with fun. Or freedom. Sarah wonders how she ever came to be. She looks down at her ageing hands and sees the imaginary stain of tobacco appear briefly on her fingers.

"You looking after a grave here?" the girl asks.

"No. Not exactly. Like to, but I can't," Sarah answers.

The simple directness of the girl surprises her. No one has ever asked her before. It was as if it never happened.

"Sorry, I just thought . . ."

"That's alright. I just like to come here. Sit. Think. Bring flowers. And you?"

"I lost my baby. Premature. Too tiny to live."

"Ah, the little mound of raw-earth down there."

Sarah feels the needs to comfort this girl, tell her that she too has lost a child, and that the passing of time makes things easier. But she doesn't tell her the whole story or say that grief is no less raw with the years.

Eldon had been so different from her father. He was alive with energy and possibility that she fed off. She knew he had a wife and a young son: but she didn't care. Despite what her parents said and what Eldon pressed home from the pulpit, he didn't make her feel the slightest bit soiled. She just couldn't help herself and neither could he, despite him having God on his side. At eighteen she thought that anything might be possible if you wanted it enough.

"You married?" the girl asks.

"No. Never," Sarah replies. "You?"

"No. On my own. A right shit, he was."

"There's a lot of them around," says Sarah. "Even back in my day!"

Sarah drifts back to '68. Smiles at how things were said to be changing. Back in Station Road things weren't about to change any time soon. The phrases *shame on the family, either it goes or you go,* are echoing down the decades. She recalls that day soon after the argument with her parents when she takes her new-born baby with its cap of red hair and its pale skin to the caravan. She liked the feel of it there on the edge of the moor, isolated. She would shun as she'd been shunned. It was her and Evan then and a living to be earned now that a future in university had been ruled out. No one ever visited her and Evan there. Not even him, even though he was just steps away sometimes. And she never went to Hermon again. *Fuck God.*

In the early days, she propped Evan in a papoose on her back as she hooked up the trailer to her brother's old Land Rover, working with the rhythms of nature; the approach of daylight, the ebb of the tide. The donkeys and the horses were fewer then, and there were not so many women out the sands and those that were still there turned their backs on her, muttered things beneath their breath. She used to drive down to Salt Point and follow the hoof fall of ponies and the tracks of tyres as others had done over centuries. She'd trudge along the vast expanse of ooze, negotiating the gouges of the pills, until she parked in the space left by the retreating tide.

Sometimes as she was hunched with her rake and her riddle scratching for the cockles beneath the surface of the grey-brown mud, she felt it was God's punishment for being tempted by the devil. *Thy will be done.* Other times, she was sure she could hear the cockles singing for the joy she had with Evan as they'd open their fluted pink shells in some heavenly synergy, filling the eerie landscape with music.

She had to watch the light. And the tides. They were fast here and she was often working with her back to the flow. *Keep close to mammy,* she used to say, as Evan grew and did his own digging with a little rubber spade and bucket with red and green swirls on.

And then one late August Day, the Bank Holiday, just before he was due to start school, she turned and he was gone. She could hear the sound of her own scream inside her head, hear it reach a crescendo and hear it fill the whole of the Burry Inlet, echoing through the void that had been created. They all banded together as they did back then, a community of cocklers, the men and the women of the sands, calling out: *Evan, Evan, Evan,* and driving their beaten up old Land Rovers through the slime. But there was no knowing where and how deep the suck of the quicksand was or the shifting trickery of the snaking pills. And the tide was racing, faster than the time they had left.

Be not deceived
God is not mocked
for whatsoever a man soweth, that shall he also reap

❧

The two women sit a long time on the bench, bonding in memory and loss. The clouds that hung on the horizon earlier have come in with the advancing tide, along with a wind from the south-west that has whipped up the water in the estuary. Everything is now hidden beneath the sea. The cockle beds, the pills, the cord grass; you wouldn't know what lay beneath the surface. Only the marsh ponies stand motionless, fetlock high in the salt water, facing shoreward in a stoic acceptance that if they stand and wait, the sea will retreat when the time is right, and things will be as they were before.

But that's just horses. Sarah says her goodbyes and tells the thin young woman that she hopes she sees her again one day. It's been nice to talk to someone and sorry she has to leave, but she's expecting someone later and has to get back. Then she rises from the bench and makes her way back slowly back to the caravan as if by rote. She likes the feel of the key in the lock: the comfort of its turn, letting her back into her familiar space, everything where it always is, where she's put it. The light is fading fast and she switches on the table lamp and takes a book down from the shelf and tries to settle herself down to read until her visitor arrives. She can't understand why she didn't tell Richard she was having a visitor when he'd joked about it earlier.

The rain is nailing down on the metal roof of the caravan. Above the din, she hears a car draw up in the yard. She'll make it quick or else she'll have Richard over. She doesn't get many knocks on her door. This isn't like Richard's distinctive pattern of fingernail against glass, like a bird's claws. This is knuckle against aluminium. Determined. Confident. Just like his father. She gets up from the settee and makes her way to the door. Why she is feeling uneasy, she doesn't know. She's had more to deal with than this in her life. With trembling hands, she unclasps the chain from the door, pushes back the lock and opens it to see the grown-up version of the little boy back in Hermon, the physical incarnation of a name that for a short time in her young life was as familiar to her as Evan's. He's on the step, a sorry sight, drenched through.

"Hello, Sarah. It's good to meet you at last."

When he opens his mouth, it could be Eldon again, the deep tone, the neediness of it.

"Come on in, Michael. There's a terrible state on you," she says.

In the light, Sarah sees a man now, middle-aged, slightly older than her Evan would have been, give or take a year or two. It's not just the voice that's Eldon's; it's the red Penclawdd hair, the navy-rimmed, pale-blue eyes; and the hands which feel bony, smooth-skinned and sensitive, as she reaches out her right hand to shake his.

"Let's take your coat, you're soaking wet. I'll put the kettle on," she says.

She watches as Michael sits down on the very edge of the sofa as though he can make a quick exit if things don't go well. He places a large envelope he's brought with him on the floor.

"Thank you for responding to my letter. Didn't know what to expect," he says.

"I was sad to hear about your father . . . and your mother. Sorry for your loss," she says.

"He wanted you to have these letters," he says. "There are quite a few as you can see."

"Always was one for words. Like his sermons. Shame he never posted them though, isn't it?"

Michael doesn't answer.

"Never mentioned me or Evan before your mother went, then?"

"No, but I had a feeling there was something."

"Something, eh?"

"He just seemed to go into himself after Evan was lost and Hermon closed. And then they moved away to the city. A shadow of himself."

"Must have been *really* hard, for him," she says. "But at least he had his God."

"Turned his back on it all – after Hermon."

"Ah . . . *Fuck God!*"

"Sorry?"

"*Fuck God*. Hermon. It doesn't matter."

"Anyway, he just wanted me to give you these."

He places the large envelope onto the old coffee table. Sarah can tell that job done, he's anxious to be off. And then the messenger is gone again, out into the filth of the night. Sarah sits up into the early hours just looking at the envelope, thinking; though has no interest in reading its contents. She'll deal with it in the morning.

My tears have been my food day and night,
  while they say to me all day long, "Where is your God?"

❧

The day breaks full of promise. The cold front has pushed through overnight. Sarah opens the doors and windows to let some air into the caravan before she starts on her daily cleaning ritual. Even the world outside looks as if it has been washed clean; baptised. The late summer light of early morning is gentle on the estuary almost without shadow and the water limpid, like milk. It will be a good day for a walk

She sets off as usual, her bag on her arm, to take her daily constitutional down a weed-choked country lane. She forges forward, feeling younger than she's felt in an age. She doesn't stop at Hermon, *Fuck God*, but heads out the sands.

The tide is even lower at this time today, and the cocklers are hard at it, speckling the horizon far out. But close in, she's quite alone. She delves inside her bag and pulls out a tiny hand rake. She stoops and starts to scrape the sludge back to form an oozing pile at the side of the hole she is creating. Doing this erases the time between then and now, though she aches more these days. When she's done, she reaches over to pull out the envelope from the bag. She rips it once, straight down the middle between the long edges, and twice between the short edges, and three times, and four times and lays the tatters in the open grave she has made. She kneels at the side in the mud and glimpses fragments of his self-pitying words blue-inked on the paper, smudged with what were probably tears. But her ears are filled only with the sound of Evan's young voice and the joy of cockles singing.

IN SEARCH OF THE PERFECT WAVE

I T'S STILL DARK. In the dead cold of a December morning, Sam switches on the small fit-for-purpose lamp attached to his woollen balaclava to illuminate the inside of the Beetle: winter wetsuit, helmet, sex wax, towel. He does a mental inventory, as though he was at work; he can't leave anything to chance.

Everything is there, in place, ready for when he leaves the lab later. He can't afford to waste any time. Time is more precious than ever these days, especially these short days of winter. Even working flexi-time, leaving at three, doesn't allow much daylight. Whether there's a six-foot swell and perfect waves or just a messy shore break, he can't allow himself to miss a minute in the water.

His short board and leash are secured on the roof rack, lashed down with bungees as the Beetle growls out of the village. He couldn't imagine living life away from the sound of the sea's roar. The sticker on the back windscreen, *surfers do it standing up*, fades into the distance as his wife and baby daughter still sleep soundly.

He tunes into Radio 4 for the 6 a.m. shipping forecast. It's looking good. He whoops out loud at the wheel. *Lundy, Irish Sea: Winds south to south-easterly 3 to 4, veering easterly later. Fair.* He anticipates the surf conditions, sees the beautifully-shaped waves rise up before him, clean faces, peeling off to the right, holding up in this offshore wind, not too strong. The tide will be right too: he knows them by rote, from his careful study of his bible – the annual time-table from PJ's surf shop in Llangennith. Once he gets to work, he'll ring PJ for the daily surf report to double-check his instinct. He needs to make sure that it will be Llangennith that'll be working later, can't bear the thought that he'll hear the gloat of the other surfers saying: *You missed it. You should have been here, man.*

Perhaps this is why he's known in the surfing community as Sad Sam because of his passion for the sea. Even though he is almost fifty, the pull of the ocean has not weakened: it still beckons, summer, winter, whenever.

Shortly after three o'clock, he's back in the village. Vicky, his young wife, and daughter Molly are at the window, waiting for him to come home, listening for the throaty VW engine to approach, the only noise to break the silence of the village on a winter's afternoon. He imagines his wife saying: *Daddy's coming, Molly. Listen.* But instead of pulling into the drive, he just slows down, lets the engine tick over, and waves to the two distant figures peering out through the window. Then he drives on, accelerating through the narrow lanes that lead to this Atlantic-facing beach, into the car park adjacent to the giant sand dunes at Hillend.

Jacket off, tie off, shirt off, he stands on a towel taken from the boot at the front of the car, breathing in the smell of neoprene. He talcs his neck to ward off wetsuit rubs and wraps the bin liners over his legs and arms to make it easier for his wetsuit to slide on. He can't see the surf from here, but he can hear it. It sounds wonderful. Different today from when the usual south-westerlies make a slop out of it, albeit sometimes a mighty slop. He can hear its power booming across the expanse of sand. It's an hour before high tide. He can sense perfection. He sees the marram grasses on the dunes cower uncharacteristically towards the sea with the power of the wind off the land. Yes, the waves will be holding up well, keeping their shape. He kneels on the frosted grass and waxes down his six-foot short board with the sex wax; breathes in its distinctive perfume, more exotic than any woman. He fleetingly thinks of Vicky though rarely of Molly. He inserts his ear-plugs, trying in vain to halt the growth of cartilage across his ear drum. He is adapting, mutating, becoming a creature of the sea. They call it surfer's ear.

Helmet on, board tucked under his arm and he's away: bounding from the car park, scaling the face of the sand dune in front of him at the pace of a man half his age and then racing along the board walk and down onto the beach. It never ceases to amaze him, this beauty in front of him. The winter sun is low in the middle of the bay, and a deep red glow turns the sea a dense, almost surreal, tone of liver; the spray blowing towards the horizon, like a white ruff.

He can't bring himself to believe in God, any god. Doesn't fit with his scientific discipline; but standing alone on the shore, facing seaward, makes him want to believe in something. It's always been so difficult to communicate this feeling to anyone, especially to Vicky. There is a sort of communion between him and the sea. He is at one with nature when he's on his board, he tells her; but she'll never understand. Never stop being threatened by it, as though it were another woman.

He sizes up the ocean, decides he'll go in at what the locals call Three Peaks, mid-way between Diles Lake and Burry Holms. It's always quieter there, you don't have to fight for space, don't have to holler, *My wave*, and claim it for yourself ahead of all the other surfers, black-rubbered seals, competing for a wave, watching and waiting, always waiting to catch that perfect wave. There's a sand bank there, a few hundred yards off shore and it produces a fast ride that thrills to the core.

He walks towards Burry Holms and wades into the water. The chill pierces his body and he pees, warm urine filling the constricted space between his skin and the rubber skin of the wetsuit. It's what being in a womb must feel like, the comfort of amniotic fluid. With his board under his arm, he dives head down into the oncoming wave. The cold shocks the system, shooting pain in the teeth and head, like eating ice cream. Later his forehead will be blue. But that will be later. The feeble rays of the sun attempt to stop the cutting cold; but it doesn't matter that they don't. He's fighting his way, paddling outside now, head and chest raised off the board, hands slicing in unison through the water, diving through the clean walls of the waves that are coming through in sets, hard and fast upon each other.

And then he's there, alone in the lull of ocean far outside the sets and the shore break, astride his board, looking back at the land from a different perspective. There are no problems here: life's issues are rinsed clean. Here he's free of the difficulty he has with his breathing from time to time, free of the niggling weakness in his chest, free of the debilitating bickering of a failing marriage. She'll come round, see his way of thinking, one day. Or perhaps she won't. He doesn't care either way.

He rises and falls with the gentle undulations, looking over his shoulder, waiting for the right set, that certain wave he'll go for. He goes for the first, up onto his feet, crouched low, knees bent, right foot forward. He's always ridden goofy-footed. The wave is unfurling to the right and he's up, hurtled along by the momentum. But it dumps and carries him almost towards shore again in an agitation of white froth.

You can never have enough of this; it is a gnawing hunger, deep in your gut that cannot be satisfied, he tells everyone Even though his body aches more these days, and the battle from the shore to get outside seems to become harder, he goes on believing that the next wave will be the one, the wave to end all waves, the perfect break that will propel him right in a perfectly poised and balanced balletic dance, white spume above his head, tubed in a tunnel of ecstasy.

The sun drops into the ocean like a burning stone before that wave comes; but there will always be tomorrow. As he treks back along the beach, the wind in his face, he marvels at how wonderful Gower is. Such compactness. Such a variety of sea conditions that it's almost possible to always catch a decent wave somewhere. If it's blown out in Rhossili on the west, in a force 7 or 8, you can always find shelter and a cleaner wave in Oxwich on the south side of the peninsula, or round the Holms at Broughton. Life is good when he keeps this in focus.

She's waiting at home for him. It's dark again by the time he has unloaded the car, hosed the salt off his wetsuit and hung it up to dry, ready for the morning. With Molly in bed, she is pacing up and down in the hall, waiting, just like Sam waits for those waves. She's spitting at him, her voice high-pitched and needy.

"You don't know what it's like, cooped up in this God-forsaken hole, on my own all day, with a baby to keep amused."

"Look Vicky, you wanted the baby. Not that I don't love Molly, but I always said, if you have a baby, it'll be your job to look after it."

And then it's the same old nightly record: Vicky telling Sam that he's not normal, Sam telling Vicky that he has no wish to be. Then it's the selfish issue, Vicky playing the Molly card and trying to load Sam with paternal guilt. Sam realises that Vicky will never get it: that surfing's not a hobby but a way of life. He'd made it clear to her before they got married and he intends to do it till his dying day. End of story.

He would always be married to the sea.

🐚

Come spring, Vicky and Molly have left. He takes advantage of the evenings that are drawing out and his new-found freedom. Nothing to get home for now - no long faces, no barbed words - he can stay in the water for as long as he likes, when he likes. He surfs Llangennith as often he can when there's a good swell and the waves aren't dumping. He sometimes surfs Langland - Crab Island and the Reef - but as a city beach, it's often too crowded with exuberant youth clamouring for a wave; and it's here he feels it again, but this time it's stronger.

He's in the water, sunlight dappling the surface, which is warming up now that April's come. He's gasping for breath. It's never been this frightening before. Heart. It must be the heart, he thinks. Just like his father. Or stress. Delayed reaction. Whatever it is, he must get out of the water quickly as the tightness is gripping him. Perhaps it's asthma or a chest infection. Thoughts race through his brain as he paddles to shore and is beached up on the sand, spent and exhausted. He feels vibrations in his thorax, a constriction in his throat, an inability to swallow. Panic attack. He's heard about people who suffer these. In, out, in, out, nice and slowly now, try to regain breath. He lies on his board trying to relax. And the moment passes.

There are no more of these attacks throughout the spring or early summer, but by July they come again, intermittently, only when he's exerting himself in the water. He's a scientist, it can't be much; he feels and looks so fit. Perhaps muscular, he thinks. It's the weakness that is the most terrifying factor, and the possibility looming that he will not have the strength to make it to shore when the attacks come. He can't ignore it. He'll see a doctor, though he won't take pills, pour chemicals into his body. If it's stress, he'll overcome it the natural way. Yoga. Go see a homeopath.

He gets the diagnosis in September, just as the autumn tides are at their highest and surfing conditions are perfect – four to five-foot swells and a gentle off-shore breeze. His intellect finds it hard to accept; apart from the occasional blips in the sea, he has never felt fitter. How can an athlete like him, his body honed to perfection, his diet one hundred per cent pure, his heart rate, slow and steady like a drum in his ear, succumb to something that had never occurred to him.

The Saturday the clocks go back is a glorious autumn day: crisp and cold. The sand at Langland has a dusting of frost over it, right down to the water's edge. Sam treads slowly across the whiteness, his rubber boots leaving impressions in the sand-frost, disappearing as he reaches the limestone rocks. He feels so well, though there is a weakness now right down the left side of his body and he tires easily with exertion in the ocean. He's ditched his short board now and his flashy nose-riding on the Reef or at Crab Island: leave it to the youngsters, the able-bodied.

The weather gives him a feel of euphoria, the adrenaline pumping through his body as he tucks his long board under his right arm and treks out to Saga Point – where he'll meet up with his cronies, the mostly over sixties, who surf gently on the slow, easy-going waves off the headland. Of course, he hasn't told them, doesn't want their sympathy. He'll carry on while he's able.

He picks his way across the jagged, pock-marked and barnacled rocks until he's at the stepping-off point. He smiles and gives the guys the thumbs up. He's going to enjoy this. He throws his board into the water and dives after it, attached by the leash. It's deep here outside the shore break, and he's never known the water so clear. Must be the stillness as there's no sediment and he can see all manner of life beneath the surface: shrimps, crabs, sea anemones. It's so beautiful he is overcome with joy.

He paddles out beyond the point where the sets are rolling in and waits and waits. Perhaps it will be today, that perfect wave. He watches the other guys take their chosen waves, admires their style, their grace, hears them yell with the rush of it all as they cut past him. But still he waits for the right moment. He hears it before he sees its magnificence. It's almost a roar. He turns straddling the board and watches it approach and as it draws nearer, he jumps up and takes position. He gets carried by the momentum of this long and languorous wave, tubing above his head, carrying him endlessly across the bay.

SOME PEOPLE LIKE
THEIR FISH TO TASTE
MORE LIKE CHICKEN

GREG LOVED FISHING though didn't like fish to taste like fish, but more like chicken. As for his taste in women, I had no idea. There was an Alice doing cooking ready for Christmas, back indoors in his ground-floor ocean-front condo. He said she liked the heat back where she came from in North Carolina and her blood had thinned since she'd come south in May. She chilled easy, even in the sunshine of a Floridian day in the high seventies. He said she liked it in the kitchen.

He looked time-warped when I set eyes on him for the first time, on the beach that December day. I'd not seen a man that shape since the seventies: an inverted triangle on two lollipop sticks, no flesh on the bones, knotted arms, toasted brown as a walnut. I remember thinking how every boy I knew back then – mostly surfers – seemed to be built like that and it took me back momentarily, not in an unpleasant way. He was so at odds with the mass of white blubber that seemed to blob around wherever I looked.

I'd presumed he was a surfer. And from a distance, I'd presumed he was young. There was a lot I presumed in those first few moments of seeing: drugs, booze, a string of women – there was obviously a toxic mix of pleasure and adrenaline that was keeping him so skinny. But close up, I could see he was older, though how old, I couldn't tell: his face lined, his lips thin, and a few wiry grey hairs sprouted round his dark nipples which I noticed didn't match the full head of lustrous hennaed hair that hung down past his shoulders. I wondered why he bothered to dye just the hair on his head and not on his chest. Obviously, not for Alice who got to see him all over. He constantly hopped from one foot to the other with some kind of nervous energy as though he was hoping to stave off the descent of old age. He skittered back and forth along the shoreline to check his rods the way the sanderlings skittered beside the frill of ocean. They'd come south for the season; they'd milk it for all it was worth. And then they'd fly back north.

I learned quickly that he wasn't a surfer, even though he wore a shark's tooth around his neck. Despite the swells and the offshore winds and perfect breaks, it was just the fishing. For days before he introduced himself to me, I'd just sit in my beach chair above the strand line and observe him. He always seemed to be there ahead of me however early I took up my lazy position. Each day he'd have a different rod, each day he'd wear a different pair of baggies; but the folding white chair was always the same, the green cooler box that housed the bait was always the same, as was the pink bucket in which he'd place his catch.

I found out for myself after a couple of weeks the difference between fish that tasted like fish and those that didn't: the ones that were more like chicken – the bass, the pompano – white meat, delicate, just right for eating – that were harder to come by. These were the ones that would be cradled gently in Greg's hands, flaunted to walking passers-by, before being

placed in the bucket full of brine. The others – the fishy-
tasting fish with the strong tang and the dark meat – the Jack
Crevalles, but the Blues mostly – were cut from the hook
and dumped back in the shore break. Some were tickled –
or taunted – I couldn't tell – just under the chin so that
they'd utter a croaky frog-like sound. Greg told me that they
were pleading with him to be put back in the water – which
he mostly did. Though I could not forget the one he left
crumbed with sand, to writhe till it gasped its last. Even
though it was no good for eating, it was good for bait, to lure
the kind he liked. So he took his knife and hacked through
the shiny, skinned fish, staking the newly-dead meat to his
hooks and tossing the head with the eyes still sparkling to the
waiting pelicans.

⁂

Like the snowbirds, I flew back north once December had
passed. Despite the fact that it was to an empty nest now that
my children had long grown-up and gone and my husband
had died, home beckoned. Sometimes I felt like a shearwater,
thought that I must have an invisible magnet implanted in my
brain that pulled me back to my very own limestone headlands, year after year. I missed the greyness and the miserable
drizzle of Gower; I missed the permanence of my little village.
I needed to bed in again, though I didn't know what rooted
me, stopped me from moving on.

But the strange, thin fisherman had unsettled me somehow
in a way I couldn't put my finger on. We'd shaken hands,
embraced in a European way and exchanged business cards
that last day on the beach, and that was all; yet I found myself

thinking about him. I imagined Alice still there in the kitchen serving up love food for him when he'd done with his fishing at the close of each day.

❦

He turned up without warning. He stood outside my front door with a small kit bag and a guitar case under his arm. He'd let himself drift north on the Gulf Stream, he said; and this is where he'd been washed up, on the opposite side of the Atlantic. I took him in out of the south-westerlies, which seemed to be bending that fleshless body of his to snapping point, and into my kitchen. I'd fix him something to eat, try to put some meat on his bones, just like Alice. I stood over the heat of the Aga, face flushed, wondering if he'd take to my cooking as he took out his Gibson from the velvet-lined case and started picking at the strings. He played left-handed, plucking with just three fingers. He told me he'd been doing this for six weeks, but I didn't delve into what had happened. I sensed he didn't want to talk about it and it was none of my business after all.

It was the first time I'd seen him fully dressed and I was drawn to the pale snakeskin cowboy boots with pointy toes that he wore over his jeans. He could make that bass guitar talk and he told me he was still much in demand in reggae circles, jamming around the Jensen beach area of Hutchinson Island, though his big-time days of gigging were over. It was then I understood why he dyed his hair and kept it long in the Rasta style. I carried on searing the fish: it was local bass, white and meaty, a fish that didn't taste that much like fish, but more like chicken. I hoped it would be to his palate.

He wasn't a beer man or a wine buff; more of a cocktail person. He fixed me concoctions I'd never tasted before: margaritas, lemon drops, tequilas. The ingredients were just sitting there in my booze cupboard; they'd just never been put together like that before. I sipped the sweetness through the sea-salted rim of the glass; it was new. I liked it. His tanned face with its sharp bones and his magenta shirt brought a touch of somewhere else to my slate-flagged kitchen with its black granite surfaces.

Outside, the rain beat monotonously against the window panes. Inside, I wanted to get under his skin, find out more about this stranger who'd come north searching for something. Or perhaps he was escaping something. He made me feel youthful again, full of lust and a wobble in my gut made it difficult to eat. It was ridiculous for a woman of my age, but I was jealous of his past, the hundreds of groupies who must have chased him down. He laughed when he told me of the Tiffanys, the Melissas, the Britneys, but he never told me the name of the girl who became the mother of his child. It was a long time ago, he said, and now he just wanted to make love, make music, fish and live on the beach. He'd been lucky enough to find Alice, she was a good woman, kind and loving, and she'd managed to put 8lbs on him since they'd met. He said she stuffed him full of homemade cookies, blueberry muffins and rum balls. I couldn't compete with that – I was more of a savoury person.

We stayed mostly indoors through the winter, apart from walking to the beach and back. He didn't suit the greyness of a Gower landscape. It seemed to drain him of colour. I didn't want to court gossip in the village either, though I imagined the tongues were already wagging on scraps of information that would be doing the rounds. They'd all presume some-thing, and have something to say: their jaws well-oiled just waiting to fuel the vitriol about the merry widow at Bay View and the dark, long-haired hippy who'd come to service her.

For a man who was comfortable performing in public, when it came to sex he seemed shy, even a little gauche.

"Do you mind if I turn the light off?" he asked.

At first I thought he was being sensitive to me: it was a long time since I'd let a man see my body.

"How about I light some candles?" I suggested, thinking that with his past, incense might appeal.

"I'd just like to be with you in the dark," he said.

And during those cold days, we loved like blind people, high on the touch, smell and taste of each other.

꙰

When the days lengthened and it warmed up, he seemed to come alive. I asked him if he felt bold enough to make an entrance in the village pub. He didn't seem to understand what I was talking about, didn't realise he'd be summed up in a second in the nod of a head, the glance of an eye. I didn't understand either, why I was doing this, venturing to a place I hadn't set foot in for over twenty-five years. I just wanted to for the sheer hell of it.

Mostly it was full of blokes. They stood propping up the top bar set aside just for locals in the very same position as I'd left them all that time ago. Men now. Older. Atrophied. Still hunched over their pints of dark with a lemon top. Others were seated around a couple of small copper-topped tables, the surface swilled with bitter, not much conversation happening, just the synchronised shove of a pint glass to the mouth and back to the table. All looked up and turned their gaze to us as we made our entrance through the door with the blue velvet curtain drawn across the inside.

Poor Greg was not versed in pub protocol. I tried to explain that it wasn't really like the slick and charmingly-run bars in Hutchinson Island. He sat on the settle while I went to the bar after I explained to him that I'd *get them in*, this first round. It didn't take long before the interrogation began. At the bar, my back was to Greg and I presumed I was out of ear shot.

"What brings you out then, Meg? Been a while," he said.

Of all the people I didn't want to be in here it was him, Joe Bevan, local farmer, from whom I'd had a lucky escape before having the fortune to find my late husband.

"Showing off our latest catch, are we?" he went on.

"Don't know what you're on about," I said.

"Him, over there on the settle. Hiawatha," he went on.

I could feel myself getting hot now. Angry. Embarrassed. Protective even.

"Won't go far 'round here in those high heels," he taunted.

"You don't change, Joe, do you?"

"Meaning?" he asked.

"Bloody bigot. Still on your same stool spouting the same shit."

"I'm just saying, not your type really, is he?"

"Don't have a type," I hissed under my breath before just looking over my shoulder and signalling to Greg that I wouldn't be a minute.

"Be careful, that's all I'm saying. Just wouldn't get hitched up with a bloke that wears snakeskin cowboy boots with high heels and pointy toes."

"Careful? Stuff your advice. You're in no position to give any. But I'll give you some. Never mess with a woman you'll never marry because there'll be no kids, 'cos if you dare do what daddy doesn't want you to, he'll cut you out of the farm."

I'd said my piece. It had taken twenty-five years, but as they say around here, *the truth will out*. I turned and took the few steps back to where Greg sat. No one had joined him on the wooden settle to say hello. We sipped our cocktails – Small Fry the bar man had even dressed the glasses with little yellow umbrellas – but we didn't talk much, just watched. He told me that he thought there'd been a little more atmosphere from what he'd heard about village pubs. I laughed and said this was Gower not some gentrified, theme-parked village in the Cotswolds. The talk was not often social, more about the price of diesel, foot rot and mange. We didn't stop for a second drink, but left though the blue velvet curtain, the men nodding their heads as we did.

We wound our way home, along the narrow track that was now bursting with yellow gorse and the heavy scent of May. It seemed hard going for us in the silence that had fallen, even though everything around was alive and full of promise. The pub seemed to have sucked the words right out of us. As soon as we got back in the kitchen, Greg sought comfort in his beloved Gibson. I recognised the chords instantly. McCartney. The original left-hander.

"This is my favourite track ever," he announced. "Know it?" And for the first time he started to sing:
Baby I'm amazed at the way you love me all the time
Maybe I'm afraid of the way I love you.
"Know it? Love it!"

And I sang too. More than sang, I screamed from deep in my gut the way I'd heard McCartney scream to a crescendo in '69. It was a cacophony. Tuneless. Primeval. But I was compelled to let it out like never before in the ordinariness of my kitchen with a man I didn't really know.

"Long time ago, eh?"

He sighed as he put down his guitar.

"Yes, funny how music takes you back, makes you really feel as you were at the time. A bit like dreams, I suppose. But sadder," I said.

⚜

When summer finally arrived, it was worth waiting for. They said in the village it was even hotter than '76. It was a time of unfamiliar landscapes: we trekked across the normally lush green grasses of the burrows, parched and yellowed by the fierce and endless heat, to reach the beach where the soles of our feet burned as they touched the sand, hot with the sun. The sea was like bath water and Greg looked in his element as he stood in the shore break, the sea caressing his calves in a familiar Floridian way as he cast his line out, over and over again, his bucket at the ready on the sand. The bass were in close; we could see them jumping. But as in Florida, it seemed they were trickier to land than the stronger-tasting fish that Greg didn't have any interest in: shoals of mackerel that darted like silver, splintering the limpid surface of the ocean beyond the waves.

We'd squeeze every last drop of light out of the day, barbecuing our catch outside on the patio as we downed ice-cold beers, for which Greg had developed quite a liking. I began to notice how quickly he quaffed the first pint, how he'd put his mouth down to the frothy head and slurp noisily; how he'd lick the white scum off his top lip with the tip of his tongue. His drinking pace would quicken with every pint, and the more he drank, the less care he took with his food. I had often thought how sensible Americans were with their cutlery: cutting it all up first with their knives and forks and then just using their fork in the right hand to eat; it was just the *way* Greg did it. He slashed his fish and then stabbed at it with the fork in that left hand of his, troughing it into his mouth. I hadn't realised he was so loud in his eating habits: chomping on the bread, chewing with his mouth wide open like a cement mixer, talking the whole time without taking breath. He'd pick up the crisp skin of the fish and crunch loudly and then, one by one, he'd place his greasy fingertips in his mouth and suck them clean. I watched intently as he did this, itching to tell him off, say *manners please*, in the way I'd once told my children. I came to realise that there was a lot you could tell about a man in the bedroom by watching him eat his food.

He was downing beer without it touching the sides, he was getting looser and floppier somehow, as if he might open up more.

"Do you ever see her?" I asked.

"Who?" he said.

"The mother of your child."

"Zip it," he slurred, moving his left hand from one side of his mouth to the other. It all looked back to front.

"Left you, did she?" I continued.

"Bitch," he said.

"Me or her?"

"All of you." He glowered as he flicked the metal cap of yet another bottle of bitter. "Never satisfied. Any of you."

There was no point in dealing with a drunk. And a morose one at that. He looked a strange mix of sadness and cruelty sitting there in the half-light. The broken finger on his left hand came to mind again and I felt queasy.

We sat subdued as the sun slipped into the sea above the Holms. He couldn't ever imagine himself getting used to the sun setting over the sea, he said; he was used to seeing it come up over the ocean. I was glad then that the days were long and the nights were short. We turned in late and drunk and for once left the bedside lights on. For the first time I saw a small tattoo inked on his buttock: the outline of a mermaid with a green-scaled tail and long black tresses not dissimilar to his own. There, indelible on his ageing flesh, was the name he couldn't utter: Nina. I hadn't imagined him with a Nina.

Before we went to sleep, I pulled the sashes down at the top and up at the bottom to try to get some air through the room. It was stifling. With the windows wide open, the sea sounded as though it was within touching distance, just like the beach at Hutchinson Island.

⁂

It was the second week of September when he left, the same day the house martins that had been nesting in the eaves took flight too. There'd been a frenzy in the air for a few days, a sort of in-tune agitation as they flapped around and lined up on the telephone wires. I was fascinated by how they always knew, could always sense the change in the weather, the end of the season.

Greg had simply pulled out the guitar case from under the bed. It had been lying there all the time, like a waiting coffin.

He nestled his guitar in the soft lining. Then he pulled down the lid and secured the clasps. As he knelt on the carpet, I recall noticing how his roots had grown through and a good few inches of grey hair lay on either side of his parting. He looked like a long-haired badger. I wondered why he wasn't having them retouched before he took his leave. And I wondered how both he and the birds knew when the exact moment had come: that time to arrive; that time to depart. Tugged by the invisible threads of nature, they'd upped and gone. Flown south once more.

The nest clung on under the eaves and the bird droppings marked the pine-end and the path. But I knew those birds would do the long haul and fly north again and take up residence as they always did. As for Greg, I expected he'd stay back south. There he'd stand on his patch of beach outside his condo, his rods at the ready and Alice, keeping warm and cooking back in the kitchen.

Sometimes I think of him there, oceanside on Hutchinson Island, those egret legs of his, jittering from side to side. I see him always looking out to sea: reading the signs, hoping. But the image is fading – just like the bird droppings on my pine-end bleached out by the Floridian sun directly overhead. Though what I won't forget is the image of that Blue, swimming around in the face of a wave one minute, the next hooked and hacked to pieces. It was simple really, I suppose; its too-dark, too-gamey, too-fishy meat of no use, just dead flesh to lure in the elusive ones that would always taste more like chicken.

LEAVE THE LIGHT
ON FOR ME

T HE FIRST LIGHT of an April morning wakes Colin
Rees earlier than usual. He gets out of bed and treads
quietly down to the kitchen. He finds it still empty: Mother
not yet up, no table set. He lifts the stainless-steel cover off
the hot plate and puts the kettle on. While he waits for it to
come to the boil, he leans back and allows the range to comfort
him. The kitchen seems much bigger this morning with just
himself there.

The steam brings him to and he turns and pours the
boiling water. He places the pot on the warming plate, pulls
down the knitted cosy and leaves it. While the tea steeps,
he pads softly in his socks to the front parlour, not wanting
to wake his mother. Here in this room, the blinds are
pulled down, and there's the unfamiliar smell of polish and
lilies. On a trestle in the centre of the room lies his father
in an open coffin, where he'll remain for just a few hours
more.

Colin stands at the side of the casket looking at the body.
He's rarely seen his father so still; he was a man always on
the go. He watches, expecting him to move just slightly,
or breathe even. The face looks younger in the dimness of
the room: the lines seem to have been ironed out, the skin
slackened and relaxed around the jaw, and there's stubble on
the chin that looks like it has grown overnight. His father

wouldn't like being seen in public unshaven. Or without a tie. In the white, silk-lined space, he looks lost, as though death has already shrunk his frame. And the hands folded across his chest are his hands too: broad, manual hands.

Back in the kitchen he pours himself a mug of tea: strong, black, no sugar, but decides against taking his mother a cup upstairs. He walks to the scrubbed table. For the first time in his life he doesn't know where to sit, in his usual chair or in his father's at the head of the table: the polished arms of the empty carver seem wider and more open this morning. He sits where he's always sat and settles himself as much as he can, hunches over his tea and allows himself a few minutes more, lost in the fug of steam.

It is light now and time to get going. He tries not to scrape the legs of the chair across the stone flags as he gets up. He closes the door quietly leaving the warmth of the kitchen behind. Dry now, under the corrugated plastic roof of the lean-to, his steel toe-capped boots lie where he took them off the night before, and the night before that; laces loose and yawning open, waiting for him to step into them.

From the yard outside, he looks up at his mother's bedroom window, curtains still drawn tightly, and wonders how she must feel knowing that after fifty years of marriage, she'll spend the rest of her days sleeping alone, and wonders if he'll carry on sleeping alone too.

It is drizzling; monotonous grey spits that seem to soak him from the inside out as he goes in the shed and hooks the trailer to the quad. His father is lying freshly-dead in the parlour for a few hours more, yet life's going on for him in the same pattern as it always does: hour by hour, day in, day out, season after season. Leaning forward, he grips the rubbers of the handle bars and heads for the fields on the lower slopes of Rhossili Down to check the stock.

Under the blackthorn along the edges of the field, most of the lambs are suckling; but in the middle there's a heap of fleece stained red, strewn across the grass, and a magpie feasting on what's left of a carcass, bobbing its head and slurping out the entrails. Nearby, a still-born lamb, its eyes pecked out, the sockets hollow. As he hefts the weight of the dead ewe and lamb onto the trailer, and pulls away full-throttle, he rants about bloody foxes and vows he'll be out with the gun as soon as things get back to normal. He thinks about his life and whether it would have panned out differently if he'd been born with a caul over his face, whether he'd have some luck or free choice even.

He unloads the fallen stock, cursing his lot and all the regulations and paperwork. By now his stomach is growling, a hollow feeling deep in his gut and he hopes there'll be a breakfast back at the farm as there usually is. As he gets nearer, he sees there might be as the washing's already pegged out: his checked work-shirts are tails up, collars down, blown full of air.

There was a time when the line had been heavy with the shirts of men and boys: Father's and those of his two younger brothers, Mother adding more and more to the lines as the years went by. But he's the only one left now. He thinks back to all the long-gone springs when he'd be dragged out of school to help out on the planting. He can feel how his back used to break on the Gower Earlies and dibbing swedes. There were all those summers on the hay, grafting till late in the night, cutting, baling, bringing it in under cover before the rains came. He remembers the note he'd have to take to

school to explain his absence, written in his father's almost
illiterate, faltering hand: *Sorry Miss Morgan but Colin was
elping me on the ay. Yours sinseerly Tom Rees.* There were
the autumn harvests, docking mangolds and the Christmases
where the family shrunk, one by one, as his brothers left the
fold, married, got their own places. The image of the kitchen
chairs emptying stays in his head. He leashes the two collies to
the post in the yard with the orange baling twine and trudges
back to the kitchen. He unties his boots, tries to scrape off
the mud on the cast-iron boot-scraper. Always the feel of
cloying mud.

By the time he gets back in the kitchen, Mother's up and
there waiting in her place at the side of the table ready to wait
on him hand and foot: pour him tea, slice the bread, trudge
to the pantry to get him anything and everything he needs,
never sitting down until she's sure he's happy. He wonders
how long she'll have left now that Father's gone, thinks about
who could possibly replace her. Who would want to make his
bed, buy his clothes, polish his shoes, peel his spuds, blow his
nose, tell him when he needed a bath or a shower? He spreads
his toast thickly with butter and gooseberry jam, but the sight
of her wrapped in her pinny takes the edge off. The whole
life strangled out of him in this twelve-by-twelve room with
the low beams where the ham hocks hang from the hooks in
the ceiling. He can't stomach it here in this kitchen where he
sees his whole life unfolding. There'll be a wife one day, a girl
from a local farm. She'll come here, to this sixth-generation
family home, marry him, get Mother in the bargain, all the
days of her life until Mother goes to join Father, goes to
join the other Reeses now silent and mouldering under their
tombstones at St. Cenydd's. There'll be a child, hopefully a

boy, who'll grow, bring home a wife, bring forth a child. Colin sees himself here, a mirror of his father, the big-bellied wife at the side of the table.

"Better get yourself tidied up, they'll be here soon," she says.

"Aye, plenty of time. Won't take me long," he says.

He runs the bath and scrubs off the morning's muck that has browned the lines of his palms and got under his finger-nails. He looks at his hands: calloused, agricultural hands. Was he born with these hands? He looks at his body, sinewy and lean, hard muscled, even his forearms. He likes the feel of his fingers against the solid flesh. He slides his head down and sinks under the hot water, his eyes open, staring up. He makes the most of the feel and clean smell of the suds. He scrubs up well: shiny like a vigorously-scoured saucepan. His skin has a glow from years out in the open air. He walks to the bedroom, towels himself dry roughly and then buttons up his best shirt, growing tighter by the year round his neck. His one suit, which does for weddings and funerals, is pulling across his chest and upper arms, and the trousers are slightly short, showing socks between hem and shoe. But they'll all be like him, the other farmers at the funeral; they'll all look the same.

"They're here," his mother shouts up the stairs. "Get a move-on, can you?"

"Be down in a minute, now," he shouts back, taking one last look in the mirror to make sure his black tie is done properly. The reflection in the suit is not one he's comfortable with. It's as though there is something more than the cloth that doesn't fit properly.

The kitchen is full again now, his three brothers back in their chairs at the table, his mother and the wives fussing around them with tea cups and cakes and white sliced-bread sandwiches cut in triangles with the crusts off. Colin sees his dead father in all his brothers. The black suits make them more alike: the Rees noses, the high foreheads and the same V shape of the receding hairline, the odd strand of grey. But there's something different from him about them which he can't quite express; they have had the edges knocked-off and they look as if they've found what they're looking for; that they fit, are happy even. And mother has her old, dark Sunday costume on, still with her apron over the top until the last minute, and her flats: she looks small and wan as if she is being swallowed up whole by all the men in her life.

Then the hearse draws slowly into the yard. They all leave the kitchen and go into the parlour to say their goodbyes for the last time before the funeral directors close the lid the way they do on other coffins every day. Colin's borne coffins many times before, always been there for the beef and muscle that was needed when the locals needed an extra pair of hands. And two are there for him today too: together with his brothers and him, they stoop and heave the coffin with a grunt onto their shoulders. Perhaps it's because he's the eldest, or the one still at the farm, he doesn't know, but he finds himself at the front, leading the way. Manoeuvring the coffin out through the parlour door, across the small passage and out through the front door, he shoulders the weight of his father as he leaves Sluxton Farm for the last time, and helps slide the coffin into position in the hearse that's waiting there, with the glass door of the boot already open.

He takes his mother by the arm and helps her into the back of one of the family mourners' cars. The black limousine slowly negotiates the steep, unmade track trailing the hearse across the fields to join the tarmac road to the village green, the other mourners' car following. He can't remember the last time the family was all together like this, though they don't say a word sealed in the car that is so at odds with the place. He can feel the jarring in his spine as the black, elongated saloon negotiates the ruts. Despite him constantly trying to keep the track in good repair, shovelling stones and gravel, the weeds keep pushing through, the potholes deepening. In the field tight to the farmyard he sees a graveyard of rust: the debris of years in layers like strata in the landscape: Fiestas, Escorts, Cortinas – his and his brothers' abandoned cars that they'd driven into the ground on the rough track. You could always trust a Ford, he thinks. All you needed was a spanner.

Colin approaches the village and sees the men, like a black ribbon, lining the narrow road as they pass slowly by and into the village green, swamped by a sea of dark suits waiting for the cortege. The women are already seated in their pews inside the church. It's a new perspective from the back of the car: his eyes roam across to the church of St. Cenydd's with its lych gate and Norman tower, its graveyard groaning with Reeses, Groves, Tuckers and Beynons who hadn't managed to shake free of this place either; to PJ's surf shop, closed until the start of the season; to the King's Head on the other side where they'll be later – all of these buildings pressing in around the village green.

He's sure he's overheard them talking there in the pub, the other farmers, slouched over their pints of dark at the bar. Behind his back they call him all sorts, he's convinced: *Mammy's boy, tied to her apron strings, queer as fuck, be careful not to stand with your back to him. Farmer, be buggered? Nothing but a lazy bastard.* They'd guffaw then, the coarse laughter of men who'd become pack animals with the drink. Though they'd slap him on the back when he came in, get him a pint – even try to get him pissed – he always felt like an outsider and the words stung.

In the church, he feels drilled by the hundreds of pairs of eyes that have turned out for the funeral to give his father a good send off. They'll be on him all the time from now on: watching, waiting, seeing what kind of a farmer he'll be when the old man is not around, seeing what he'll make of it on his own. He can sense them behind him; almost feel the foul, warm breath on the back of his neck from where he sits with his mother in the Reeses' pews at the front of the nave. For the prayers, he goes down on his knees on the tapestry kneeling mats stitched by long-dead Reeses' hands, and though he doesn't believe in God, he prays hard inside his head, though doesn't know quite what he is praying for.

It's raining again as they slide through the churned-up mud in the churchyard for the lowering of the coffin into the water-logged earth. One by one, each family member throws a handful of soil onto the coffin before the villagers file past and do the same. Side-by-side, his mother and brothers line up and take shelter under the carved roof of the lych gate, oldest to youngest, in the natural order of things, just as the shirts had been on the washing line way back, to let the well-wishers shake their hands and kiss their cheeks before they'd plough into the pub opposite.

His mother sits at a little round copper-topped table in the top bar and drinks tea, weak and black, with the brothers' wives and the village's women. She says a polite no-thank-you to all the offers of a dry sherry or a whisky and soda. And before long she wants to get out of the pub, away from the stench of alcohol and back home where she feels more comfortable.

"Stay you," she says to Colin. "Stay with your friends. I'll be alright."

"You don't mind?" he asks.

"The boys'll take me home. They've got to get back. No rush."

"Leave the outside light on for me," he says. "I won't be late – but don't wait up."

The only woman in his life leaves him there then: the day has taken it out of her. With Mother and his brothers gone, he stays, drinking at the bar with the stained-glass window in the little top room, kept open just for the locals.

"Another pint of dark for Colin," one of the local farmers says to the barman.

The barman places it in front of him, the head of froth lapping over the rim of the glass. He leans over and bends his head to suck the excess between his lips. He feels he is already becoming his father, not yet bedded-in in the soil opposite.

"Colin boy, how you doing? Takes a funeral to bring you out, then?" says Ricky, from Lower Muzzard.

"Busy, Mun. Been just me on my own up there – no life in the old man for a good while."

"Aye, sorry."

"Aye. Thanks."

"Be lonely up there with just the old girl. Time to get a wife, boy. Get stuck in."

"Aye. S'ppose."

"Another pint?"

"Aye, don't mind if I do, thanks. Dark, it is. Lemon top."

"Seeing anyone at the minute?"

"No, not at the minute."

"You?"

"Chris' no. Too picky, me."

"Could have sworn you were courting that girl from Kennexstone?

"Aye, saw her for a while."

"Smart piece. What happened there, then?"

"Don't know. Didn't feel right. Not cut out for it."

"What you or her?

"Both of us I s'ppose."

"Thought you were keen there, boy."

"Tidy girl. But no good for the farm."

"No work in her then?" Ricky says.

"No. Just couldn't see her there, that's all."

"Spoiled, you are. Looking for someone like your mother."

"P'raps. I don't know."

Ricky gets the drinks in and the evening fills with the talk of farmers: what'll happen to EU funding and set-aside now that the idiots have voted out? The price on red lead, how there's no money in fleeces anymore, better let the bastards lie in their winter coats than spend out on shearing, whether the TB man's been round and how many have gone down this time. About time they culled those bloody badgers and what about Morgan Parry, Cook's Well, left his wife after all those years and gone off with a man from Llanelli who drove a lorry. Who'd have thought? Who the fuck would be a bloody farmer? The empty pint glasses stack up on the bar. For once, Colin feels he's having a good time in the company of men of his own ilk. He hears no talk tonight, no insults. He feels included, one of the boys, and he doesn't put it down to the booze.

"Ian Taylor, Kennextone's got himself a good one, mind," says Ricky.

"Good what?" asks Colin.

"Woman. Not much to look at but plenty of work in her," he says.

"Where did he find her, then. Not round here?"

"Aye, right here. Gillian. Barmaid. Last season. Where've you been, Colin? You need to keep your nose in. Get out a bit more often. Think she was sniffing around for a farmer, mind. Swansea, she's from. Got a cousin. Tell you what, I'll put a word in for you."

"Aye. Do that."

"And remember, I'm always around, propping up the bar if you fancy a pint mind. Get you out of that bloody house for a couple of hours."

There is a last orders of sorts: the bell rings and the landlord makes the call for getting in that last pint. But it's April, and soon after eleven, the barman slides the bolt across and draws the velvet curtain. Lock-in begins.

Colin is tanked-up on the booze, feels it sliding down easy tonight, not touching the sides, and as the booze flows so do the words. He's part of something here. For a few hours he thinks life's not that bad after all. There's worse things he could be doing.

It's way after midnight when he slumps over the bar, slurring at whoever's left, whoever's listening. Echoing in his head he hears them talk again. Vicious talk. Cutting. *Lazy as fuck, eh? Queer sod? Not him. He'd show 'em all one day.*

Staggering off the bar stool, he sways to the door, loses himself behind the faded blue velvet curtain and is out into what's left of the night. He looks up towards Sluxton there somewhere in the distance, high on the down above the village, but can see no gleam. It's all in darkness. There's not a car on the road at this hour; just the stars and a full moon buttering the sky. Yet the ripe moon is so brilliantly yellow-white, orbed in a frosty halo, that the surface of the road home is lit up like a golden thread.

CHASING THE SHADOW

I PICK HER up at 7.30 a.m. She's at the front door ready waiting for me, as though she's just as afraid of keeping me waiting as I am of being late. Seeing her like this so early in the morning, almost colourless, makes me realise how old she's becoming: her hair white, her complexion wan. She seems to be being bleaching out before my eyes. She limps to the passenger side and I wonder if she's up to the trek that's ahead of us. I get out and say I'll help her in, but she snarls back that she can do it herself, thank you. I should have known better than to ask. Still the same Mum. She smells like an old person as she closes the door and seals us in the car together.

"Hair looks nice, Mum. Had it done?" I remark.

"You don't like it, do you?" she snaps.

It seems longer than the fifteen minutes from her village of Landimore in the north of the peninsula to where we park up in the field the farmer's set aside in the south, at Middleton. She talks about what's been happening in the village: who's dead, who's dying, who's moved in, who's moved out, without really *saying* anything. She rarely asks me a question and if she does, she doesn't listen to the answer.

"Enjoy the sponge I sent down with your father last week?" she asks.

"Lovely," I reply. "Different from the usual."

"Apricot filling. *Good Housekeeping*. Thought you'd like it," she goes on. "I'll send down some soups for the freezer with him next week . . . squash, leek and potato, carrot and coriander. Should keep you going for a while."

My mouth says a polite *thank you*. And yes, they'll keep me going for a while: the scraps of home-made food she feeds me every fortnight without fail, to stop me starving to death.

"Make sure you give your father the sponge plate back when he comes down. I know you think I'm a funny bugger, but I can't help it. My mother's, you know. And the Tupperware containers when you've finished the soup," she says.

"OK. I'll make sure," I reply, incensed that she always wants something back. "Be nice if you came down with Dad now and again, Mum. Bring the food yourself," I say.

"You're always busy down there. Don't want to make a nuisance of myself. Believe me no-one knows more than I do how it is with working from home. Or have you forgotten?"

"No. I remember, Mum," I say.

"And anyway, I don't always feel like it, you know, a bit up and down these days," she says.

Every day for as long as I can remember she's been a bit up and down. Taken to her bed every afternoon, assuming the horizontal. But I don't say anything as I hear my father say: *now don't go upsetting your mother, she hasn't had it easy, you know. Try and understand.*

And I do. I know she hasn't had it easy: losing one mother to TB when you're only two is hard, even tougher to find mother number two dead in a bath of cold red water with her throat slit when you're only a young mother yourself. That's when she started the long, slow countdown. Waiting for death, I called it, but there was no way she'd ever see anyone else's point of view, least of all mine. Me, always the difficult child according to Mum because I was born on a Wednesday, and dragged into life with the aid of a forceps.

I see her now with her thick mass of sliver-white hair and recall that time when her periods stopped overnight and her lustrous freshly-washed black hair that always smelled of Vosene fell out revealing a patch of pink scalp the size of a half-crown. I must have been about thirteen, I suppose, when I felt she left me the way her mothers had left her. She might has well have been a sepia image in a brass frame lined up on the mantel piece with the other two dead ones. Death row, I called it not so long ago; but she didn't laugh.

"Better get a move on," I say. "Need to find a good spot and get ourselves set up ready."

"I've made some sandwiches," she says. "Nothing fancy, just a bit of cheese and pickle. Know you like those. And I've got the Thermos in the bag. You don't mind carrying it, do you?"

I take the two folding canvas chairs from the boot, the blanket and the bag and we set off out of the field to pick up the path to the cliffs.

"You going to be warm enough in *that*?" she asks, or criticises, I can't be sure. But I say I'll be fine. Even though it's the 20th March and the sky is cloudless for the moment, there's still a nip in the air.

We make our way slowly across the fields that are deeply rutted from the tractors and I fear she will fall in the brown-red mud, and that it will be my fault. She picks through the caked cow pats and I offer her my arm for support, but she ignores it and ploughs on. I can see it's such a struggle for her to get over the stiles with the pain in her lower back, and she curses the new-fangled kissing gates that have been put here recently; but she's making the effort.

We are the only people around on these south Gower cliffs

this special March morning. Unpeopled, this landscape forged from limestone appears even more spectacular: upended cliffs, faulted and fissured, jutting out into the jaws of the Atlantic which today is in full swell and an offshore breeze holding up the faces of the waves, spume blown back to sea. You can feel the past here, breathe in the remnants of ancestors, taste that trickle of time.

The sun is still low at 8.15 a.m. We close our eyes, raise our chins in unison and let this first hint of gentle spring warmth caress our faces. We set up our chairs side-by-side on the grassy tussock as close to the edge of the cliff as we can. I feel dwarfed here by the power of nature: on my right is Mewslade Tor and beyond that, four miles of folding grey rock to Worm's Head. On my left is my mother, set against the backdrop of Thurba Head. It's a powerful combination, a perspective I'm not used to seeing. I congratulate myself that I've chosen well: this is a perfect vantage point. You couldn't ask for a more wonderful setting for the dramatic scene that will soon play out here. The grass is sappy under our feet and silver webs of dew cling to the blades; rabbits scurry about oblivious of our presence; gulls wheel above us and guillemots call out from the cliff ledges and overhangs. Everything is full of promise.

"You took your first steps on these cliffs," she suddenly says. "Twenty without stopping. After that you never looked back."

"You've never told me that before," I say. "How old was I?"

"Eleven months. Walked before you talked. Very independent child . . . Anyway, I've got us these glasses," she says. "Your father ordered them online for me . . . keep our eyes safe. He said we'd be better off with a colander – you know what he's like – but I insisted. They're one size fits all."

She hands me a packet and takes one herself and we tear open the packaging. Inside we each have a pair of solar-eclipse glasses: black oblong lenses to filter out all the harmful ultraviolet and infra-red, surrounded by a thick card frame decorated with swirls of hot crimson, orange and yellow, like the surface of the sun as we imagine it to be. She puts hers on first before I do the same, hooking the thick arms around our ears and nudging the card to fit as comfortably as possible on the bridges of our large Bevan family noses. We look at each other in our identical eye-wear sitting in our identical chairs and see the funny side. I'm conscious of our strange, almost girlish laughter, filling the emptiness of the surrounding space.

"D'you want a sandwich?" she asks. "I'm going to. Can feel my sugars dropping."

"We've only just got here," I say.

"So?" she says. "There's no rule to say we can't eat. You've always been such a stickler for things."

I take a bite of sandwich and chew on it and her words, and vow I'm not going to be drawn in. Not going to spoil the day. We sit munching in silence, looking out to sea, waiting for it to happen.

The wildlife senses it before we do. There's an agitation in the air and a flapping of wings: a frenzy that normally comes with approaching dusk. The gulls still and disappear I don't know where, and the buzzards circle overhead on the thermals before disappearing with the rooks into the spiky blackthorn and the bramble of undergrowth. The rabbits run to ground and a growing silent presence spreads over us like our heavy blankets. Under the hedge that separates the wild from the tamed fields behind, a new born lamb jerks to its feet and latches on to its mother's teat. We watch without words as the sky darkens second by second, and the grass seems to lose its greenness. Dark shadows roll across the clifftop mottling the heath, as the moon begins to swallow the sun, bite by bite.

"Powerful thing, nature," my mother says, as though to herself.

We gaze at the sun's surface for as long as we can, safe behind our glasses. Every few minutes I glance at my watch and my mother. These moments as the moon passes between us on earth and the sun are not simply about the skies darkening and sharp edges being obscured in soft shadow, but about how many kinds of dark there are, how subtle the tones of light to shade. There are all manner of changes afoot. It's not a total eclipse at our particular fix on earth, 51 degrees north, 4 degrees west: at ninety per cent it's deemed only to be partial. But it's dim enough for me to realise what it could be like when the moon blocks the sun out completely and utter darkness descends. It's the cold that I feel most; damp cold, chilling me second by second as we approach 9.30 a.m. and maximum coverage. I tug my blanket up around my chin; tuck myself in as I did when I was a child. I reach for my mother's wrinkled hand and for once she lets me take it. It lies soft and unfamiliar in my grasp. For the next few brief moments we focus on the ten per cent of the sun that still remains shining, a small but bright crescent that hangs on in there like a strange grin on a skew.

JUST IN CASE

ON THE FIRST evening, it is only a snatched glimpse through the open window of the car. Fleetingly, its amber, wide-eyed stare holds mine just long enough to feel that it is making some deep connection.

As we drive the last few hundred yards home along the single-track lane that leads to our house, I feel its eyes pierce me still; and I am filled with disquiet. I close the door to the half-dark world that has unsettled me, flick on the light and switch on the television, and take comfort from the blabber of characters unknown to me.

"What's up, Aggie? You've gone quiet," says my husband. "Are you ill or something?"

"No, I'm fine," I lie. For there are no words to convey this sudden and inexplicable shift. He is by now used to fluctuations in my moods and perhaps this is just a woman thing. He's wiser than to pry further and with no more questions, wraps me in the shawl of his arms, far from the other-worldliness of the last half-hour. Temporarily, I feel lifted.

But when night comes, broken sleep fudges the boundaries between the real and the imagined. I am running along the freshly-painted broken white lines marking out the centre of a road. They are reflecting a sickly light across my face. I can see my pallor under the moonlight. There is no traffic, just me alone in my flimsy cotton nightdress. The landscape is familiar to me, not far away at all. I recognise every curve of every bend, every incline, the overgrown hedges at the edges of the road that I skim with the tips of my outstretched fingers as I journey on; though I don't know where I am running to. There is an aching heaviness in my limbs, perhaps because the wind is impeding my progress: an unusual direction, off the land, chilling my cheeks. My lips feel parched; on my tongue there is the taste of metal. Just when I think I can run no further, I sense it there behind me, hear its slow wing beat, before it takes me in its talons and lifts me high into the sky, gripping me safely in the hook of its beak as we glide forward together to who knows where.

I find it difficult to get back to sleep after this. By day a rational individual: by night, a believer in superstitions, soothsayers, even my mother's old wives' tales. *Things come in threes.*

The next day breaks bright, laced with frost and I dust off the debris of a disturbed night and the gloom that cloaked me the previous evening. It was only a white owl. It was just a rare sighting. I busy myself with my work in the studio, never ceasing to be amazed at the views I breathe in: such vast open skies and vast open seas – uninterrupted vistas of the three-mile sweep of sand between the limestone prom-ontory that crawls out in to the Atlantic like a worm and the tidal island of Burry Holms that twice daily rises like a turtle out of the sea. And in March it is unpeopled, magical, and all mine. Sometimes I could feel almost blessed if it wasn't for one thing. But, I don't talk about that anymore, not now.

This same evening, beyond the dusk, before the dark, it seeks me out. It is the second sighting. It sits in marbled stillness amid the bare branches of wind-crippled blackthorn at the edge of the field. But tonight the air is quiverless and the bird bathed milk-white by a rising moon. It swoops low, its wings full-spanned, stretched wide in all their feathered lightness, in all their creamy whiteness, hovering, searching, dipping over the hedgerows and the acres of stubbled fields which roll almost to my front door. It is as though it is demanding admittance, wanting to come across the threshold, for me to invite it in. In the half light, I notice that the fine hairs on my forearms are standing on end as its eyes fix mine.

It has followed me home; I know it. This same owl I saw that first night. It is surely coming to me with a message. I realise how little I know or understand; only that I feel bonded to this creature in some mysterious communion. I can no longer keep my misgivings to myself. I beg my husband to explain what he thinks the significance of this owl is, to bring the logic I crave to the situation that has come into my life.

"Why do you always have to look for deeper meaning in things, Aggie?" he say. "Why can't you just accept things at face value? It's just an owl, for God's sake, it's after voles and vermin, not you."

"Then why haven't I ever seen an owl here before, in all the twenty-five years we've lived here?" I argue. "Let alone a white one. And not once, twice now."

"You Celts," he says, "you're all doom and gloom, not happy till you're crying and drowning in your own misery. D'you like being unhappy, or what?"

"I'm not unhappy," I protest, "I'm just unsettled by it, that's all."

I wonder at that moment whether it's fear, or just fear of fear that's made me the person I am, but I know this white owl will return once more. There will be a third time.

I lie in bed, restless, anticipating – perhaps even willing

– that characteristic screech or midnight hiss that owls make, to begin. My mother has often told me old Welsh tales of women who take their clothes off and put them back on inside out to stop an owl's hoot. Or of those who hurl salt, hot peppers and vinegar into the fire in the hope that the owl will get a sore tongue. But outside all remains calm. It is only inside my head that my mother's words knock against my skull: "Things always come in threes. Take it from me, I know."

Dawn wakes me early, forcing itself through the peep in the curtains. It is still before 6 o'clock and I am sleep-heavy, my breath sour, that metallic taste on the tongue again. Lack of rest has made me queasy as though a million butterflies are fluttering inside me. I swing my legs over the side of the bed and feel the need to steady myself. I want light and open the curtains wide to allow the day into my bedroom.

The view that meets my eyes never fails to amaze me. But this morning it almost overcomes me. I put the emotion down to poor sleep. The burrows are brushed with the burnished bronze of sunrise and the conical dunes, a lunar landscape, sharply defined and stark with shadow that will lift with the rising sun. This depth of feeling I have never experienced before. It is almost like illness. Like misery, my husband would say. And I acknowledge silently that he is right; that I cry when I feel at my happiest. And I feel over-full with an unexplained emotion and notice that tears are spilling from eyes and I hadn't even realised.

As the day dawdles by, the euphoria passes. I know *my bird* will return this evening. There will be a third time. It's out of my control. I can sense my husband's irritation: "For God' sake, Aggie, get a grip, he says. "Look, it's new day, cloudless, almost perfect. What more could anyone want?" We are both silent then, neither of us daring to utter the one unspoken word that could answer that question.

Of course it comes the third time: a muted wing-flap in the dying sun. The land is pink-tinged, smudging imperceptibly into the bleeding sky. Against this canvas, the owl sweeps and swoops at full span, its ivory plumage almost touchable it glides so close. It is the silence that is so shocking; such a big bird, yet it is strangely noiseless for reasons I do not understand. Other lesser birds are frenzied at this just before dusk time before they settle for the night. But this owl is serene; so silent. It circles above and then it does what I know it must. It comes to within inches of me with its message. I read its eyes, startlingly bright in its flat, heart-shaped face. It connects for what I know will be the third and final time. And then it is gone into the long spring shadows.

Now that it has gone, there is only the waiting and the honey-tipped feather it has left behind. Days, weeks, one month, two months, three dread-filled months, yet nothing. But my body and mind still do not accept the nothingness and I merely exist in a constant agitated state of expectation that won't go away however hard I try.

I wake habitually early, dizzy, my head spinning. My husband tells me that I am not myself, that I am off-colour. He wears his concern on his face like I wear my sickly mask. He attributes everything to my over-active imagination, a Celtic pessimism and the damned owl. He doesn't dare mention my hormones; he's wiser than that.

I've grown to accept endings over the years, that fate did not deal me the cards I desired. I have become immune to the never-endingness of impossibilities. I have learned by now not to dare have hope and have grown wise to not dwell on the tell-tale signals of loss: untimely blood spots, the cursor pointing to an empty void on a computer screen, all those silent heartbeats. But at forty-five, the idea of possibility seizes me. It could just be. When I begin to tell my husband what is happening to me, I watch his expression change. It says that his menopausal and barren wife has finally gone over the edge: deranged by full moons, old wives' tales and visitations of white owls at sundown. But I plead my case. There has been no monthly bleed since the beginning of the year.

I insist he climbs into the loft and brings down the Moses basket that has been stored there for almost half a life time: *just in case*, as my mother would say. I tuck fresh white sheets over the tiny mattress and place the single feather in an empty crib.

EVERYTHING YOU NEED
TO KEEP YOU BUOYANT

E ARLIER, THEY LET themselves in with the heavy iron key that's been left for them under the geranium pot in the gravelled courtyard. Out of the intense June light, the shuttered kitchen is dim and cool. They're pleased to see the wicker welcome basket groaning with produce on the granite work top, smell the air thick with the smell of pink garlic, ripe peaches and cantaloupe. Two glasses have been placed ready along with a bottle of local Gallaic rouge, which they uncork immediately, a sweet mix of fruit and spice escaping the bottle.

A little later, once they have settled in, they sit on the terrace, at the table with the familiar red, plastic cloth and gorge on strong hard cheese from the Tarn and hunks of bread, and toast the week to come. It is dark by then: rural France dark, though the air still hot and humid. The grating of cicada legs summoning their mates, provides the backdrop to their conversation.

"You OK?" he asks.

"Yeah. Fine. Good to be back," she says.

"And?" he asks.

"Just as it was," she replies.

They decide the dishes can wait until morning before mounting the twisting stone staircase to the bedroom. The blistering, blue shutters have been thrown open and put on the hook when the luggage was taken up, the windows flung wide in the hope of letting the outside into the stifle that's been building up over the day. The cotton voile curtains hang limp in the breathless air.

As she switches on the bedside-table lamp, she notices that the feature white-painted walls behind the bed are flecked black with mosquitoes that have eased their way in. She doesn't mention the windows to him, but takes a match and ignites the coil at the side of the bed. Immediately, the smoke curls, the smell of phosphorous and formaldehyde filling the room.

"Christ, sorry," he says, "forgot."

"Doesn't matter. Not now," she replies as she walks to the bathroom. She sprays herself with DEET, rubbing it deep into her skin before putting on a pair of old pyjama bottoms in the hope of protecting herself from the bloodsuckers that seem to be attracted to her; always it seems just her. She cannot bear the thought of the angry wheals, the ongoing itch, the distorted ankles and wrists she'll suffer if she's not careful enough. The pyjama bottoms will also do to cover the jagged scars on both knees, still livid even though it's almost a year now.

He's asleep by the time she's done, flat out on his back, snoring loosely. He's never had trouble sleeping, even after it had just happened. She watches him closely, one minute wanting to place a pillow over his face, the next wanting to run her fingertips across the downy hair on his cheeks. She wonders why, wherever they are, he claims his stake to *his* side of the bed. He has to, he says. The right side. The driver's side.

Sleep doesn't come easily to her anymore. Deep into the night she remains propped against the plumped-up pillows, taking in the bedroom. From this perspective, it looks as it always did: high above her the hewn timber beams supporting the roof, laden with dried lavender; the honey-coloured stone of the walls; the large cheval mirror with the gilded edges looming there. Apart from the mirror, there is only the overly large bed with the white duvet and the two identical fans on chairs either side. She attempts to regulate her breathing as she's been shown: in one, two, three, four; out one, two, three, four. And when she feels she's ready, she puts out the light and allows the monotonous whirr of the motors and the cool air brushing her face every few seconds to soothe her in the sealed darkness.

෯

As first light leaks through what little gap there is between the shutters, she reaches her arm out across the bed in the hope that the holiday will make him lie in a little longer; but there is only an empty space on the cold, base sheet and a hollow depression in the pillow.

She creaks along the floorboards to open the windows, but it's only a wall of warm air that hits her, so she hooks them up again firmly to try and maintain at least some control over the temperature inside. She wasn't expecting this heat, doesn't know if she'll be able to take it.

On the terrace he's already been busy sorting breakfast, and is still clattering around with crockery and glasses, setting the table with fruit and fresh baguettes.

"Bonjour," he says beaming, and kisses her on the lips. "Sleep OK?"

"Fine," she says.

"Going to be a scorcher. Look!" He walks to the giant thermometer hanging on the wall and points his finger. "Twenty-eight in the shade. And it's only seven."

But she only half-hears him; her eyes have shifted upwards to the immense wooden crucks supporting the red-tiled roof. She hadn't noticed the spikes before: scores of them, metal, mean, rising menacingly from the horizontals. Now it makes sense, why it is absent of birds seeking crumbs, why the feral cat that lives in the wood shed doesn't bother coming.

"Only one place to be on a day like this," he says.

"OK with me," she says.

He sets up a lounger for her under the striped awning by the pool in the untamed part of the garden by the perimeter of the field next door. There was a time when she'd loved the sun, had staked out on tin foil from dawn till dusk, slathered in olive oil, constantly basting and turning herself in tandem with the intensity and movement of the sun. Now she lurks in the shade, in its shadow, feeling so exposed in her bathing costume: her white and wasted thighs; her bottom without muscle; the scars on her knee caps like large purple-red ferns that don't see the light of day.

She should feel lucky that she's alive, she supposes, rather than fret about the superficiality of appearance. After all, she's been told often enough how fortunate she is to have come off so lightly. How simply awful it was for her husband, they'd kept saying, how terrible for him to come to terms with what he'd done, to have to live with it for the rest of his life. It must have been simply shocking for him to be breathalysed in the middle of a hot August afternoon, for the police to ask his next-door neighbour if everything was alright with his marriage, for him to witness the air ambulance taking her away.

She watches him immersed in his novel; some crime thriller or other. It doesn't seem like it is that hard for him to get on with his life, there are no visible scars. She looks at him and is washed over by anger. She sometimes gags on the words that are just sitting in her mouth waiting to be spewed: "You stupid, bloody idiot! Why didn't you see me? Why didn't you even fucking look?"

"Fancy a swim?" he asks.

"Not right now. Reading," she replies.

The sun is hotter that she ever thought possible. It pierces her half-healed, splintered cheek bones, giving a new sensation where until now, there was none. Only a numbness. When she raises her head from her book, through her semi-shuttered lids the world looks bleached out and fuzzy. The white and violet dog daisies in the borders around the pool hang their heads, wilting in the parched soil: there's the murmur of a strange, dry wind off the land as it rushes through the olive trees and swishes through the scorched, swaying grasses. It sounds just like the day it happened.

And on and on he swims: front crawl, breathing every second stroke, same side, the right side, up, down, up, down, lost in the monotony of his peculiar rhythm.

"One hundred," he shouts as he touches the wall at the shallow end.

Well good for you, she thinks.

"C'mon. Have a swim," he keeps on. "You used to love to swim."

"I can't," she replies. "The wasps."

There are scores of them honing in at the rim of the pool, hovering over the water that's been splashed on the tiles with the fervour of his swimming. Where the stainless-steel steps descend into the pool, they are at their densest: a frenzy of yellow and black, swarming above the puddles. The noise is incessant.

"You didn't used to be afraid of wasps," he says.

"No," she says.

"They won't sting. They're just thirsty."

"Really?" she says.

"More afraid of you than you are of them."

"What makes you so sure?"

"Look, I'll get them away for you."

And he raises his arms out of the water, flailing them around, dousing water over the terracotta tiles and the menace of wasps looming there.

"You're making it worse," she shouts, "stirring things up. Just leave them alone. Let them be."

❧

Daily the temperature rises. Religiously, every morning he checks the level of the red mercury in the thermometer on the terrace – 29, 30, 32, 33 – announcing the increases with a childish exuberance. There had been a time when his little-boyishness had been refreshing. She wonders just how hot it could possibly get without something exploding. Even the elusive, wild tabby has left the scorch of the wood shed and is stretched out languorously on the steps of the terrace, one of its hind legs draping limp over the treads. Though the space is still devoid of birds, it comes now, more sociable, its habits changed, in the hope of a bowl of water, the odd scrap or left-overs from the table.

After breakfast, she makes the daily trek along the gravel

path to her place under the awning. In the full glare of the sun, her ankles look pale and puffy, the skin stretched tight like her gran's. There's a nagging tightness in her chest too, which she feels is down to more than just the heat. A feeling of being stuck, being dragged down, drowning even. They said it would pass with time.

Every day is just like the last and the next: him swimming – 120, 140, 200 lengths – her sitting on the lounger watching the ritual, her eyes like antennae, fixed on the wasps crazy with thirst at the water's edge. She wonders why he never gets bitten or stung, is irritated by his apparent immunity. Sometimes she'd like to see him fall victim, note his reaction. Her reaction. But then it passes.

They don't speak much. She tells him it's the heat sucking her energy, and she keeps her head down in the short story she has been reading all week though can't remember much about, only the image of a woman who wakes from a nightmare, goes downstairs to the sitting room where the furniture is perfectly arranged, upends the lot, turning everything on its head, creating utter chaos where there had once been calm, before going back upstairs to bed, refreshed.

She longs for the cool of the water, to immerse her shoulders under the surface, lie on her back and drift, let herself go, allowing the liquid to erase all track of time, all memory. But it's the wasps.

He can't settle either unless he's swimming or reading. He picks up the pool net with the long handle and plunges it into the sparkling water, skimming the surface carefully, scooping out the unfortunate hornets and the dragonflies and the biting bugs that lie there dead or half-dead in their quest for cool and drink. He sorts the deep end first, until it is cleansed of every insect. He inspects the contents of the net and then tips the minutiae squashed in the mesh into the flower beds around the pool. She watches him as he does this task, from deep end to shallow, meticulously, with utmost concentration, until the pool is purged.

"There," he says with pride, "gone. The lot of them. Come on in."

"Sorry, I just can't . . . Them . . ." she says, gesturing towards the wasps.

"I promise you they won't sting. Trust me."

❧

The days are passing, the week almost through, the weather sticky.

"This can't go on, can it?" she asks as the thermometer hits 35.

"Set to, I think. Forecast's this for the rest of the week."

"Can't take much more of this."

"You really going home without having a dip?"

"Probably," she says. "Those bloody wasps don't look like budging, do they?"

By early afternoon, she senses a change in the weather. It's dripping hot. Hazy, chunky heat that you could cut through with a knife. On the horizon to the north are low cumulus clouds, the colour of the limestone back home. She feels that if she could press them with her fingers they would have mass, form, texture, would depress to the touch like her injured cheeks did when it happened. It had been just like feeling ripe figs

And the wind is from a different direction now too, wilder

by the minute, whipping up the desiccated leaves that have blown under the awning. This wasn't supposed to happen. But even so, the wasps show no sign of giving up the territory they have colonised; they seem drunk on the headiness of it all. She wishes that the sky would burst, shatter this oppressiveness.

The light is changing fast, and he looks different: darker, more shadowy, somehow surreal through her polarised sunglasses, slicing through the water that is now without sheen. The first specks of vertical rain start to prick the pool's surface, sending out concentric circles from where they pierce. It's beautiful rain, she thinks, convectional, mesmerising storm-rain that means business. She ponders the fact that it wasn't predicted, that it has come out of the blue.

And with the rain, the wasps are gone.

"No excuse now," he shouts.

"Suppose not," she says.

He's up and out of the water in a second and skips into the pool room where all the paraphernalia of fun is stored: beach balls, foam noodles in cyan and magenta, plastic arm bands, water wings, floats and lilos, everything you could wish to keep you buoyant. He drags a pink plastic contraption over the wet tiles and plops it in the water.

"Pour madame," he says, holding out his hand, inviting her to take her place on the inflatable armchair bobbing gently in the shallow end.

"It's ridiculous," she says.

"I know. Get on."

She leaves the lounger and for the first time in almost seven days walks to the steps. The rain is beating down on her shoulders, washing away the stored-up heat of her body and skin. She turns and carefully negotiates the steps one by one, gripping the rails, the water lapping over her calves, her florid knees, her waist, her chest.

"Get under, it'll be lovely when you're in," he shouts.

She knows he's right. So she takes a huge breath in, closes her eyes, and plunges her head deep under the water. She keeps her mouth closed, opens her eyes and holds that breath for as long as she can. As she resurfaces she sees his expectant expression, willing her on.

"I'll steady it, hold on with your hands and heave your body up. I'll keep it close to the edge," he says. "Trust me."

"Don't laugh. Promise you won't laugh," she says.

"Promise."

But he does. They both do as she falls off time after time and is submerged, making a rude rubbing noise of flesh against plastic, until she finally slithers on to her stomach and inches up the chair, getting her balance and then turning onto her back. She can sit up straight, support her back, as this beast has arms and a head rest and even a place where she could put a drink if she wanted one: for she knows he would get one for her. She only has to ask.

She wallows in the cool of the water, letting it lap over her legs, the rain showering her face and arms. He swims close, encircling her, keeping a constant eye on things. Just in case. He bobs up out of the water from time to time like a baby seal to kiss her knees. She reaches out and strokes the top of his greying hair. Their laughter sounds strange to them against the rumble of thunder in the near distance.

ON THE FOURTEENTH DAY

ALMOST TWO WEEKS after it had happened on that unexpectedly hot May Day, Richard Morgan was still to be seen sitting where he'd sat almost every day since. He made a forlorn figure, solitary and motionless in the sand dunes, slightly obscured by the marram grass which seemed to mirror his stillness. His eyes were fixed far out across the expanse of Rhossili Bay. Or at some place far beyond.

Down down in the deep blue sea
Catching fishes one, two, three

There'd been a change in the weather almost immediately after it had happened: it didn't seem fitting somehow that the sun should continue to blaze, or the sky remain blue. It demanded a sympathetic response from the elements themselves. And it was then that a cold front had pushed in off the Atlantic and punished this west coast with venom, uprooting trees and upturning caravans. Take that as well, it seemed to screech. And ever since this force-8 south-westerly had abated, it had just drizzled – a monotonous Gower-grey drizzle, soft and almost without sound.

Despite the ferocity of the storm, nothing had been churned up, nothing revealed along this vast and deserted shore. During daylight hours, when he managed to raise his body from the sand, Richard Morgan had walked its length after each high tide, checking the flotsam and jetsam along the high-water mark with the eyes of a gull, for what the sea might bring to shore.

There'd been the debris he'd normally expect: planks of wood, bleached white by the salt water. There were stumps of trees, strangely sculpted by wind and water that to Richard Morgan resembled mythical beasts – a unicorn, a phoenix. As he walked, he trampled across swathes of bladder wrack, crispy in parts under his feet, but also squishy black pods that he still felt compelled to pop between his fingers. One by one, he popped them, with a satisfaction and comfort that surprised him. And there were the sad mermaids' purses, designed to protect the eggs of the young, which lay marooned on the tide line, doomed to perish. He picked up a conch shell and pressed it to his ear, hoping.

And there were things he didn't expect: bizarre items that had intrigued him. Mounds of red elastic bands littered the damp sand; the unwanted cargo of unseen ships, like dead worms spat out by the retreating tide. He raged out loud on the unpeopled beach at the sight of detergents in large plastic containers with Spanish labels, spent contraceptives, an old armchair, resting comfortably in the wet sand facing out to sea, and streaks of black sticky oil, flushed out secretly from unseen tankers. He raged out loud at the empty ocean.

Death shrouded Richard's thoughts: starfish, once peachy and fleshy, lay desiccated, drained to pure white, their five-limbed symmetry disfigured. He pondered the wonder of their missing arms and their ability to grow them back; a resurrection of sorts here on Earth. Portuguese Men of War washed in on the Gulf Stream and the precocious warm weather lay stranded, bulbous and translucent, their fine, red blood vessels visible through the blue-whiteness. An image flooded his mind of children in summer – laughing and jumping on them as they would a grotesque bouncy castle.

Strung out along the frill of ocean, there were dead fish, their once shiny scales, silver and streamlined, now stripped of that glint of life. And those eyes just staring at him. Just staring. The stench of sea-death made him retch.

Down down in the deep blue sea
Catching fishes one, two, three

⁂

Up at Headlands, the white house that bravely stood full-frontal to the elements, Meg Griffiths and her husband Dafydd were blessed with the wonderful aspect of the sweep of the bay in its entirety, from Worm's Head to Burry Holms. That May Day the view had been breath-taking.

As dawn had broken, the ocean had taken on a mantle of deep blue, fringed pale pink at the horizon. The sky was clear apart from the occasional wispy cumulus that didn't look threatening at all. As Meg looked out from the bedroom window, the terrain had such definition that it seemed she could have stretched out her fingers and touched it. The burrows had looked strangely lunar, their conical peaks tinged plum in the early light, the black shadows deepening the hollows between them. She listened to the breeze hiss through the long grasses and watched their gentle morning dance, and gazed as the herring gulls drifted effortlessly high on the thermals, like specks of white vellum parchment. It was beautiful. Perhaps too beautiful.

By lunch time the sun had bleached both the sky and sea and they seemed to meld into one another, fuzzing the horizon. That week had been one of spring tides. And with the pull of the full moon and the strong off-shore wind, there had been a sizeable swell – not that an outsider would have known. But Meg had lived here long enough to know these things, feel them even.

And it was on this day that Meg had talked to Dafydd about ominous feelings and strange sounds of the sea – *thunderous, hollow sounds*, she said. Even though it looked calm and non-threatening, she talked about *rogue sets* that were breaking far outside the shore break, sudden sets that could rise from nowhere. Dafydd often joked that she was some kind of a witch, his very own Mystic Meg. He laughed and asked her if she could feel things in her waters or in a new ache of her joints. But the laughter was often to mask his fear of her uncanniness. She just seemed to know, as though she was on a different wavelength from normal people. She couldn't explain how she knew. She'd listened to the surfers over the years and imbibed their inside knowledge of the sea. She'd also lived long enough to have learned a lot of country lore from the old people and the farmers who were mostly gone now. Sometimes she would suddenly break into little rhymes about *rain before seven* meaning *fine after eleven*, or things being *too bright too soon*. There were often pronouncements about the harshness of the coming winter based on the holly or the birds, or how you couldn't pick blackberries after Calan Gaeaf because they'd been touched by the Devil.

But it was the sea that moved her most. She knew its moods, its power, its patterns. All Dafydd could see was the tip of the Worm in the distance, where the full force of the Atlantic funnelled up through the blow hole in the limestone, the spray and spume frothing cliff-high. But what Meg talked about wasn't that obvious.

Above the *strange sounds* Meg had alluded to, she could actually hear the crashing boom of the shore-break, waves which had been held up by the strong off-shore with no trace of peaks (or white horses, as the day-trippers called them) like meringues, now dumping on the sand. And then the surge back out, those undercurrents, that strong undertow beneath the surface that could be felt, but not seen.

Meg and Dafydd usually joked that on high days and holidays, some unsuspecting idiot would be caught out. Safe in their garden, they would watch the spectacle unfold. The coastguards would race through the narrow lanes to the beach on the report of someone's lilo being blown out to sea, or a kid wandering off, and the helicopters would whirr overhead, the inshore lifeboats would patrol the bay. Usually it was nothing too serious and usually there were happy-ever-after endings. But that day seemed different to Meg.

"Something's going to happen," she said to Dafydd. "Just got this feeling." And she placed her hand across her chest as if she could feel the hurting inside her already.

They sat in the garden then, warmed by the spring sunshine, and gazed out at the countless boats, specks of sparkling-white painted on the watery-blue canvas, where strangers sat gazing back to shore.

৵৵

It had had been an early start for Richard Morgan and his son Matthew, that day. At five o'clock they'd set off from Loughor where they kept the twenty-foot fibreglass cabin cruiser. They'd had it years; a *little gem* Richard had said it was, and so he'd named it *Gower Beauty*. It wasn't grand, but comfortable and equipped with a 120HP engine. It did the business for sea fishing. And that day they'd heard the bass would be in.

"Come on, Matthew, rise and shine. *Early bird catches the worm,*" he'd said.

The Loughor Estuary, usually so rough and full of chop on a westerly or a northerly, was uncharacteristically calm. As father and son had rounded the Holms into Rhossili Bay, they'd been amazed to find conditions so still. Not a ripple. So not far round from the Holms, where they knew from experience would be a good place on the ebb for the bass, they decided to put down anchor. They cut the engines, dropped the anchor, and sat on deck in just their bathers in the sunshine, setting up the bait and attaching the lures. And then they waited. Fishing was always a waiting business.

It came, on the starboard side, the undulation of the un-peaked wave, about ten foot of it, and flipped the boat to 180 degrees. Richard was thrown clear and found himself floundering in the turbulence. He swam to the boat, the bow now a roof, frantic for Matthew. But there was no sign of him. Only a few hundred yards from shore, he was gasping his last breaths while all around the sea was alive with surfers, like black slithering seals in the water, just waiting for that next set. Richard was brought to shore on a surf board; but of Matthew there was nothing.

Down down in the deep blue sea
Catching fishes one, two, three

All that evening and long after dark, Meg and Dafydd had watched the lights of the air-sea rescue glare across the bay. The day-trippers had all gone home. The car park was empty. There was not a soul on the beach, save one sixteen-year-old missing, presumed drowned, somewhere beneath the pretend stillness of the water. Meg shuddered with the realisation of what a cruel place this could be. She swished the curtains to a close across the bedroom window and shut out the night and the thoughts of that child somewhere out there, all alone.

❧

When the Bank Holiday was over, and the crowds gone, Llangennith was all hers again. So as she walked her dog along the beach, Richard had stood out as a stranger. It was the stillness that he exuded from his place in the dunes, and the colour of him: grey as a ghost. The dog ran up to him and wagged his tale, desperate to be stroked. She rushed up to Richard and apologised about the dog, but he hardly reacted, didn't want the contact. So she said good morning and walked on by. She knew what he was looking for. She knew his efforts would be futile for the time being. But she couldn't bring herself to tell him this.

With a son of her own, Meg felt for Richard. And as she watched him, she saw his child, helpless out there in the dark, unprotected, in that unknown place: a slimy blackness where there was a world they didn't know. A world that wasn't a place for innocent children. A place where you shouldn't be out alone at night, where fronds waved and trapped and dragged you down, down to the bottom of the deep blue sea where you couldn't breathe and your lungs filled and your body bloated and your hair streamed out behind you and your young flesh was gnawed.

Down down in the deep blue sea
Catching fishes one, two, three

Each successive day, Meg walked the beach and each day Richard was in the same position. Each day the dog would bound up to him in hope and Meg would have to get the lead out and pull him away. But in time, Richard raised his hand and waved to Meg as she passed with the dog, now firmly on the lead, as though he wanted her to stop and talk. She walked slowly to his lookout spot, conscious she might be invading his private space, but he smiled gently.

"Lovely dog you've got there. Must live round here," he said.

"Yes," she replied, pointing back towards the village. "That little white house up there."

"Lost my boy," he said. "Ten days now. No sign of him."

"Yes. Knew it was you," she said. "I'm so sorry."

"Just want to take him home," he said.

Meg knew how hard it was for him to speak. It was as though he had no more words left in him. She told him that she hoped he wouldn't have to wait much longer. But she didn't tell him that he'd have to wait another four days exactly.

And on the fourteenth day, Meg simply said to Dafydd:

"It'll be today. Richard will have him back today."

What the sea does not give back straight away
Will be returned on the fourteenth day

Over supper in the conservatory that night, Meg noticed

the darkening sky suddenly speared with lights. Directly in front of their house, just close to Diles Lake, the flashing blue lights of an ambulance could be seen on the scrubland. Overhead was the monotonous thrum of the helicopter as it hovered before finding a space to land.

Richard was still there waiting, sitting alone in the cool dunes, slightly obscured by the marram grass, when the sea released Matthew and washed him ashore.

Down down in the deep blue sea
Catching fishes one, two, three

EVERYTHING
AROUND HERE IS
TURNING TO RUST

R OSIE GROVE COMES-TO in an empty bed again. Dawn is slicing through the curtains. She gropes for her mobile. 06:00. God knows how long he's already been up and out. It's March-cold as she throws off the snug of the eiderdown and walks barefoot to the bedroom window. She pulls back the thin fabric of the curtains which give off a smell of must, making her sneeze. Then she clears the condensation off the glass with the back of her hand. Through the smeared surface of the pane, she looks out of the caravan across the farmyard and sees the sickly glare of the fluorescent light strips in the lambing shed.

She unscrews the catch and opens the window to let some air into the fug; the sweet-sour stench of last night's Bitter-breath still hangs around. It seems to get everywhere. She didn't hear him getting in again; must have been late. Flakes of rust from the window frame stick to her fingertips. They can't seem to do anything about it, nor the cake of salt. Everything around here is salt-encrusted or turning to rust.

"By Christ, lie down, you bastard, lie down."

Joe's voice splits the quietness she is feeling in this before-everybody's-up time. And then the yowl of the collies. The pair of them are slinking away from the shed door, bellies almost grazing the yard, tails down, straining on the orange baling twine to escape the thud of the steel toe-cap. *Lie low, boys*, she thinks. *Do as you're told, if I were you.*

Looking back, she wouldn't have done as she was told, not if she had her life all over again, she wouldn't. They said it would be a good match, marrying into the Groves; that she couldn't do much better, especially if she didn't want to leave Gower. And she didn't; the land was in her blood. She was a Bevan after all, and generations of them had farmed at Llanmadoc.

She gazes east to where the sun is rising over the Bulwark at the top of Llanmadoc Down. Her childhood home is out of sight, on the other side of the ridge; it seems a long way away from Llangennith this morning. Like two sides of a penny, the damp, north-facing village of Llanmadoc and here in Llangennith, where she was told she'd get the sun all day. She was eighteen then.

⁂

By seven o'clock, the three boys are up, charging like young heifers up and down the end of the caravan they call the lounge, making the picture frames tremble on the shelves. She snatches a glimpse of her wedding photograph. Handsome bugger he was then, all dressed up in his pin-striped suit. Gallic looking, olive skinned, a nose too large for his face, which is even wearing a smile. Eight years on and now all the kids are in school. There was a time when she'd taken *good breeding stock* to be a compliment: all that freshness, all that fertility. She now wonders who that girl in the photograph was, where has she gone? That cross between a highly-bred mare and a red-headed Celtic warrior-princess.

She's turned the boys' bed into a table by the time she hears his boots pound across the yard. He takes them off and leaves them on the step outside the door and then washes his hands under the kitchen tap. Rosie sees the water turn red, pale and finally run clear.

"Everything alright out there?" she asks.

"Shit. Bloody shit," he replies.

"Mind your mouth. The children," she says.

"They've heard worse," he says. "Two still-borns."

The children spoon their cereal into their mouths; they say nothing, but bang their heels in unison against the wooden panels of the bench seats.

"Hurry up, you lot," Rosie says, "otherwise we won't get the bus and you'll be late for school."

"Who'd be a fucking farmer?" he mouths as he bends his head over his tea, which he has black, the Gower way. He keeps his head down as his family rises from the table.

"Work hard at school, boys. Don't end up like me," he says as they slam the door and leave him alone as he likes to be.

Rosie waves the boys off on the school bus which is waiting, engine idling, at the turning space at the end of the lane. Sometimes the sight of their little faces staring out at her through the window rips at her heart. But she knows they are safe in school, out of the way until half-past three.

Walking back along the lane to the farm, she stews on the choices she has made. There were farmers and there were farmers. She'd had her chance with a Parry from Cook's Well: two hundred and fifty acres, cattle and sheep, the odd few acres of woodland too. And organic. Native flowers, the lot. But she'd feared his looks – too handsome by half in that might-stray sort of way. So she'd gone for a Grove. There'd been stories in Young Farmers before she'd married him, but she'd never believed them. Tough, yes, and she'd been impressed – wooed even – by the way he could handle an ewe. Prised between those tightly clenched thighs of his, one tanned arm locking the animal by the throat, the other making light of the electric shears, he could fleece the sheep in under thirty seconds. She'd glowed with pride when she saw him interviewed on *Wales Today*. She was happy then to be engaged to Joe Grove, world-champion sheep-shearer. But when she married him with his sixty-acres at Bank Farm, she'd got a job lot – his mother, Elsie, and his two younger brothers as well. Together they'd all shared the farmhouse. It was like a tightening noose there with its low-beamed ceilings, and Elsie seeming to fill every inch of it with her tiny, crooked frame. She seemed to be always there: in the day, in the kitchen, in her place, with her boys who couldn't do any wrong. And there, during the night, upstairs. You could almost hear her breathing through the walls, could sense her listening to them creating their own three boys in the next room. Elsie didn't look like she was going anywhere anytime soon, so they'd bought the second-hand twenty-eight footer with the rusty chassis and had it delivered on a low-loader and put in position alongside the farmhouse.

Her stomach tightens as she turns into the yard through the five-bar gate. Teetering on top of the crumbling stone-pillared posts are two identical ivy-bridled white horses' heads. She sees how the harsh elements have driven under the skin of paint in parts, revealing cracks in the concrete below, and across that once spotless surface spreads a growing stain of mould and mildew.

❧

"What time did you get in last night?" she asks. It's been there, itching on her tongue since she smelled the bedroom that morning. His breath still reeks.

"What the fuck's it got to do with you? Get off my back," he growls.

"Just like your bloody father. You'll end up like him if you're not careful."

The words seem to take on a life of their own, spilling out from her lips.

"I'm going out to check the fences around the bottom fields. Look, I don't ask much, just make sure my dinner's on the table, that's all. Less of the gob."

And with that he's away. She listens as the roar of the quad bike fades. She's got a couple of hours now to wade through the flurry of paperwork. She wonders exactly when farming turned into this paper-chase of tagging and movement of certification and TB. She often wonders if there's any way out. But you can't split a farmer from his land. *Shut up and put up*, is his way of saying it. Sometimes, especially with the drink in him, he's more adamant. But it never shows.

❧

Towser turns up just after 11 o'clock. She isn't expecting him.

"I'm here to do some servicing," he says. "Bumped into Joe in The Dolphin last night."

"So that's where he got to, is it?

"Sorry?"

"Nothing. Anyway, how you doing?"

"Alright. Nothing to complain about. You?"

"Same here, I suppose. God, it's been a while."

"Ten years. Year 11. Mr Price. Haven't changed a bit – you, that is," he says.

Rosie feels her face heat up. She didn't think she blushed anymore.

"What you been up to, then? Didn't you go into your mother's business? Food boxes or something like that?" she asks.

"Aye. Food and Flowers Are Us," he says embarrassed. "Did it for years. Died then, mother that is. Doing what I want to now. Always wanted to be a grease monkey," he laughs.

"Got out of it, then? Alright for some," she says.

"I'll make a start with the tractor and the lorry. Can sort the bike out later when Joe comes in."

Rosie watches him as he sways to the back of his truck. Lovely shiny black Nissan Nivara, stainless-steel bull bars, running boards, spoilers and over-sized headlights. The full works. Must be doing alright. He's got his own registration: TOW 10, and a sticker on the back of the cab window: *sniff my diff*. He looks different to how she remembers him from school, uglier somehow. And greasier. Long, wavy, slicked-back hair, oily skin, the odd spot on his temple above his nose, on his chin, along the panel in the middle of his face.

He carries his tools back towards her and she sees his hands are filthy, smeared with diesel like his jeans that are over-tight and bulging at the crotch. He is a cliché of a man, a pretend cowboy in coarse red-checked shirt and tan leather winkle-pickers with Cuban heels. He swaggers to the shed with an assured self-awareness, knowing that she's watching him every step of the way.

Later she takes him a mug of tea. He likes it milky, he says, three sugars. She feels that redness again as she watches him hunched over the engine of the mart lorry, his dip stick in the oil. He takes it out, looks at it, then wipes it on the rag tucked in the pocket of his hipster denims.

"You'll have a bit of lunch with us, later, when Joe gets back?" she asks.

"Aye, don't mind if I do, ta," he answers. "Don't go to any trouble though."

⁂

Meanwhile, the morning ticks by without her being aware of it. The ironing fills the space between elevenses and lunch. The monotony is soothing. There are piles of blue school shirts with their cuffs and collars, little, not-so-little, and growing-out-of grey trousers with seams to be pressed neatly, inner seam to inner seam, over and over again. She listens to the hiss of the iron, moves her strong arm back and forth, sees the creases disappear. She folds and sorts towels, socks, underwear, places them neatly on the chair, ready to be put in the cupboards in the bedroom before Joe gets back. He doesn't like to see clothes around the place, likes everything in its place where it should be, out of sight. Sometimes she'd like to leave the iron on his going-out shirt, watch it scorch, breathe in the smell of the singe, but she doesn't dare.

The stamp of his boots on the flags outside the kitchen door breaks her fantasy. He's unlacing them as she clears away the ironing board and laundry basket. She makes herself look busy at the stove: there's a clattering of pots and pans and crockery as she rushes to lay a place for him and Toswer. One o'clock. His dinner is always at one o'clock.

"Where's my dinner, woman? Don't keep a dog and bark yourself," he goads.

"Towser's coming in now. Don't mind, do you?"

"Mind?"

And he walks up to her and tugs her long hair, forcing her chin upwards. He is close to her face then, the smell of beer still strong.

"Mind? Just make sure you keep your eyes and your hands to yourself, that's all."

With that, Joe is interrupted by the rap at the door. Rosie wonders whether Towser has seen what's just happened. She brushes down her hair and arranges the cutlery more neatly. Then she stands at the side of the table, on hand, at the ready. With Towser there today, she is more painfully aware of her role: a hybrid of mother Elsie and serving wench. She wonders when she turned into this creature she loathes. She listens to the men talk. It's as if she's not there, just a tightly-aproned carcass waiting on the table. She senses that Towser picks up on her mood. After all he's from a family that's not like this. He tells them that he's got his own place now, in Llanddewi, small but nice. Joe tells him it's about time he found someone to settle down with, but to make sure it's a good one, a goer that can do the business and gives no lip. One who knows where she stands. He says the rhyme that makes the muscle in her cheek twitch:

Gower born and Gower bred
Strong of arm and good in bed

Joe says he hasn't got time to hang around all day. Work to be done in the sheds. He leaves Towser at the table. Tells him he'll see him later. Rosie starts clearing the table, scraping the plates, stacking them, carting them to the kitchen, clattering them into the sink. Feeding, farming, fucking. Feeding, farming, fucking, punctuated only by the walk to get the children on and off the school bus. She stands there up to her elbows in grease, looking out through the steamed-up windows at Joe with the black yearling.

"Everything alright with you two?" Towser asks.

"Fine," she says, keeping her back to him.

"Anyway. You know where I am. Just shout if you need me." And then he's up off his chair and out the door to sort out the quad.

She carries on looking at the yearling that doesn't want to be broken by the man planted in the centre of the shed, whose eyes she knows will be pit-black with rage, determined it will be he who will be master. Even though she's too far away to hear what he's saying, she knows Joe's words by rote: *Damn you, you black bastard, I'll show you who's boss. By Christ, I'll beat the fucking crap out of you.*

She realises that the water's gone cold without her noticing. She unplugs the sink and watches it drain away, leaving a smear of grease towards the rim. She clears up and pulls on her wellies, ready for the afternoon trudge for the school bus. She retraces her steps, out through the gates with the crumbling horses' heads, along the single-file track, past the old people's home where once a fortnight a large white van with the LLYFRGELL logo pulls up. And now, it doesn't seem likely that she'll be doing even that anymore. He'd grabbed her novel: *a heap of shit,* he'd called it, some fantasy that she'd go getting ideas from. He'd torn it up, struck a match and set fire to it outside the caravan door. He'd laughed loud and long, rubbed his hands after the doing of it, and just said: *There*. She'd felt something happen to her then. And she didn't feel frightened anymore.

The kids sit around the table while Rosie gets their tea. Joe's in from the sheds now and seems to be in a good mood for a change.

"Had a good day, then?" Rosie asks.

"Aye. Not bad. Earned myself a couple of pints," he says.

"You're not going out again tonight, are you?"

"Too right I am. Hell of a thirst on me."

The three boys stop talking and start their synchronised kicking again.

"Taking Towser for a quick one," he says. "Christ woman, we've been at it all day."

She watches the care he takes primping and preening in the mirror above the gas fire. Yes, we've been all at it all day, she thinks. He's scrubbed-up well: face glowing, hair gelled in place. She hates the way he stretches his jaw and cups his chin between his thumb and forefinger to take one last look at his reflection before polishing his shoes on the back of his trousers, one foot at a time. Then he picks up the spare caravan key from the fruit bowl.

"Towser's driving. Don't wait up."

By the warmth of the gas fire with the children tucked up, life's sometimes not that bad. It could be worse. It's what freedom might feel like, she supposes. But when the dawn breaks, the condensation will be running down the panes again and sometimes those flimsy curtains will be iced to the glass. The stench of beery breath and five sweaty bodies will hang, clagging the caravan. It will be just another long and miserable winter's day like all the others.

❧

It is still thick with darkness and cold in that just-before-dawn time when the knocking comes. Insistent; making the caravan door shudder. She stretches out her arm to where he should be in the bed. *I'll bloody kill him. Thought he'd taken the key. Kids will never go back now, not at this hour.*

"Alright. Keep it down. I'm coming," she shouts.

There are two of them standing outside, their face yellow-white in the torch light. They always work in twos, they tell her. And there's a squad car, but the blue light's not flashing.

"Mrs. Grove? Mrs. Rosie Grove?"

Apparently it must have been instant. A skid on black ice, the policeman tells her, between Kennextone and the Pancras. And no, there was no other car involved, just the Nissan, with Joe at the wheel. There wasn't a mark on him. A massive shunt to the brain. The passenger had been thrown clear of the car, which had been found by a passing driver an hour or so later.

Rosie is sure that Joe had said Towser was going to drive. But she doesn't think now is the time to think about this or say anything to the police. They are so sorry to be the bearers of bad tidings, they say, and are happy to give her the number for victim support. Whatever she needs, she only has to ask. She thanks them for some reason she is not sure of.

She goes to bed that night, alone as usual. She mouths the word *widow* time and time again. It feels soft and airy on her lips. She absorbs herself in the sensual feel as she shapes her mouth to sound the vowels. Her body is still sore in parts; she fingers the fading blue bruises on her wrists, the flesh of her thighs. She runs her flattened palm around her throat, the throttle marks shy and invisible in the dark, beneath her nightie. Her scalp is still sore after the lunchtime wrenching. Strange that someone can be dead yet their impressions remain, that the physical hurting continues.

How tragic she will appear: a widow at twenty-six with three fatherless children to provide for.

She plays the part to perfection at the funeral at St. Cenydd's a week later. The whole village turns out to see this young mother bury the man she'd married there only eight years earlier. Images of Jackie Kennedy standing in widows weeds holding her two children by their tiny hands were brought to mind as the village witnesses the most beautiful and sorrowful of sights: Rosie veiled in black lace, her hair beneath curled to perfection, tears not smearing her waterproof mascara in the slightest as she trails the cortege, clutching a single red rose to her heart, and her three infants at her side. It was enough to break the hardest of hearts. With grazes on his face and his arm in a sling, scoured clean and dressed in his Sunday best, Towser glances at her fleetingly from the pews at the back.

THE BLACK-
RIBBONED HAT

IT'S STILL HERE, you know, that black-ribboned straw
hat of yours. It's just where you left it when we came back
in after our walk around the village. You placed it on the top
peg of the coat stand in the front porch, where it hung at an
angle as though it was just about to fall off. Even now after
two years, I can't bring myself to put it straight, move it out
of sight, consider letting it go.

Today is a late-April day not unlike that one; precociously
hot, full of promise. The sun is streaming through the glass
panels of the front door and dancing on the crown of that
hat, drawing my eyes to it. I hadn't noticed until now that
the rays have already paled the straw and stolen the dense
blackness from the silk band. That's what you said you liked
about my home, the intensity of the light, how the sun filled
it all day before slipping down into the Atlantic out front. I
also remember you told me that you preferred sunset in your
other tongue: *machlud*, you said. *It means death*.

God how you adored your language of heaven, almost as
much as this place we both loved and loathed on occasion.
Not many people could understand that, could they? But we
got it, didn't we, this place that was perhaps too beautiful for
its own good. This place that you loved so much that you said
it could become you one day. But I still don't know what that
really means.

I feel the urge to stand on tip-toe and reach up and grasp your hat, feel it in my hands, but I don't think I'm ready. Don't want to feel the dryness of it, touch the woven flax that's coming undone, feel the undulations of the wide brim, worn with wear and that characteristic tug of yours. I remember how you always struggled to contain that mass of grey hair in its body as you pulled it down across that intelligent brow. Lasting impressions of you, just poised there, hanging above my head, just a fingertip away. There is a fleeting thought of placing your hat on my head, but I wouldn't dare; it wouldn't feel right. And it would never fit anyway.

You'd never left that hat here before; looking back I wonder if you knew then, had some strange premonition of what lay ahead. You were like that. A bit like the cows round here know when it's going to rain and all curl up together like commas in the field, facing the same direction. Or perhaps it was the artist in you, that certain sensitivity that tuned you in to things others could not see or feel.

Though I never referred to you as an artist, did I? Rather I always called you Geraint the Painter as though you were going to come around to the house anytime to do a bit of painting and decorating. That was the thing about our friendship, me always ribbing you to keep your feet planted firmly on the ground, stop that head bursting through the top of that hat with all the accolades you kept getting. You used to take yourself so seriously sometimes, suffering for your art. Though you knew how much I admired your work really, you'd only have to look at the walls in my hall and up the stairs to see that. There were fifteen at the last count. The final count. I don't want anymore. Not now. There they hang, watercolours of Gower from every possible angle, usually shrouded in mist, in various tones of grey. Welsh Depressionism, we called it. And I suppose that's what bound us together, our dark way of looking at where we lived. An odd couple, looking back, both of us content and married to other people, but happy with each other in our own creative misery.

I owe you a lot, you know. The way you encouraged me to write when those around me assumed I was going through another one of my fads and put it down to the menopause. But you didn't. There you'd be in your artist's get up, that hat on head, for you said you couldn't paint properly unless you had it on, and your sketch pad in hand. I'd have that little notebook of mine and together we'd be tramping over stiles and fields searching for inspiration, which for some mysterious reason we always found working in tandem. Now, without you here, I haven't been able to write a word. The blank pages of my little grey writing book just stare back at me, begging for the ink to flow. Ridiculous, you'd say. Get your walking boots on and get cracking.

There they are, at the bottom of the settle: mud-caked soles and uppers, asking me to pick them up and put them on for the first time since our walk. You had an exhibition coming up with some fancy title like 'Geraint Hopkins – the 60th year retrospective'. It was in Stow-on-the-Wold and even though you'd exhibited in The Attic in Swansea and The Albany in Cardiff, this was your first solo show over the border. You were taking Wales to the world, you said, and we were making up pretentious titles for the art-works for the catalogue: 'Broughton, rain, looking back'; 'The Burrows, fine mist, autumn dawn'; 'Diles Lake, full flood'; 'Towards Burry Holms, winter dusk'. The titles came to us as we walked, you writing them down in your jotter in that terrible scritchy-scratchy handwriting of yours for fear that they might fly away if you didn't. The titles might have been plucked out of thin air, but your work was always real. At least for me it was. If anyone could make something real, it was you. But now I'm the one who's left trying to make things up and the fact that you're not here still does not feel real.

My feet seem to propel me of their own accord to where we tramped that late spring day. It doesn't seem a conscious decision, more an instinctive muscle-memory, urging me to re-trace that route of ours. I close the gate and follow the track to where the tarmac peters out and turns into a bridle path that opens onto sheep-filled fields. You took your camera out here and snapped the old farmhouse at Carreg Wen for later reference. The farmhouse is captured in a frame now, hanging in a posh gallery in an English town in the Costwolds. For the exhibition went ahead *retrospectively*. Like your battered old hat, that word doesn't seem to fit.

I talk out loud to you as I walk: a lone woman maddened by your absence, tell you that the farmhouse has been done up since then, lime-washed in the vernacular style, and loved again by a creative gay couple who got married last summer in a tepee in the neighbouring meadow. Apparently, so word goes, they were charged an exorbitant sum by the kindly farmer next door for the privilege. There were guests there from New York, of the TV kind, drunk, kissing, having a great time. You'd have got on so well with them. I see you smile. God, you would have chuckled at what the Parish Council and their ilk thought about it.

And those caravans are still there at Broughton. *Cash crops*, you called them. I hear you tut ahead of me where I see you again standing, intense concentration etched on your face, taking another picture of the rusted anchor that stands in the middle of the aluminium enclave in the dunes. You made beauty of that anchor in the gloomy seascape of Broughton you created later, but I couldn't bring myself to buy it. There were your two signature figures in the foreground; nothing more than silhouettes, stick people, sketchy details. It was hard to tell whether they were male or female, stooped there in their shapeless windcheaters. But I knew who they were. You'll be glad to know there was a red sticker on it at the private-viewing bash. There were so many red stickers. Right now, I'd like to tell you that you were an anchor too and that I need that anchor again, that physical presence of you to ground me. But I feel mute on this one, emotions stuck between heart and voice.

You walked at a pace on that our last walk, much faster than I'm walking now. I found it hard to keep up with you as we ventured along the beach for a while, looking back towards shore and gasping at what the winter's storms had done to the cliffs: taken them in one bite. We wondered how long the benches at the top, with their brass-plated inscriptions to lost loved ones, would be safe before the ground was taken from under their feet. Among the jagged cockle and razor shells and torn feathers on the strand line, you came across a conch, bleached white and weathered smooth. You handed it to me and I placed it in my backpack. I would keep it as souvenir of our day together.

We headed along the road back to the centre of the village then; you wouldn't have known by your firm tread what was just around the corner. It was as though you had a motor in those boots of yours, powering you on. God, how we laughed when we came across the new build with the blue plaque that said nobody famous lives here yet. And as yet, no one's moved in, famous or otherwise. And then we reached The King's Head. *Ah, journey's end*, you said.

I sit at the very same bench table today on the terrace outside where we sat and supped real ale that day. It's just as it was: green umbrellas, squeezy tomato ketchup containers, cutlery in a pot, used pint glasses waiting to be collected, the smell of chips, fag ends at my feet, Small Fry the barman as harassed as ever. I feel I'd like to tell you that Gower's accolade of UK's first AONB has been hijacked and now stands for Ales of Outstanding Natural Beauty. You'd have agreed with that. I can still see the head of froth trapped in that beard of yours as you bent your head to relish that first well-earned sip. We sat and took in the view from the village green: PJ's surf shop, St. Cenydd's church opposite, Rhossili Down as its backdrop, and beyond that, the ocean.

You told me that you'd like a mooch in the churchyard and do some serious sketching. Neither of us had been there for research before, just for the funerals of our friends, which seemed to be happening more often than they used to. We stood out of the sun for a while in the lych gate for you to get your sketch pad and pencils together. Then you walked off, through the tangle of grasses to the far side where you stopped at something that caught your eye between the bell tower and the stone wall.

Your straw hat was shielding your face from the sun as you lowered yourself and bent down on one knee amongst the untamed grasses to look in close detail at a tombstone. It was overgrown with ivy and bindweed, crooked and pock-marked with time. Lichen had stained the slate and obscured the letters etched by hand. I recall you clawing at the fungus, digging deep to try to reveal the name of who'd been buried there. A couple of centuries' growth was lodged fast beneath your nails, but you couldn't distinguish anything to tell you who it was, tucked tight within that patch of unloved turf, just worn and smoothed grooves. But you knew someone was there; that someone had *been*. It was enough. You sat in silence and sketched away, oblivious of my presence. I glanced at you from time to time from the sunnier south side where I was reading the stories of those whose names were easier to decipher.

Your head hung heavy as you rose to leave for all too short a while. The breeze had risen without warning and the leaves sighed in the silver birches next to the bell tower. The dry-stone wall had cast a shadow over the flowerless plot and gulped your body whole. Your eyelids were half-shuttered, your fine features fading fast under the brim of that black-banded hat.

Today outside the pub, I feel a sudden chill on my bare arms. That breeze is getting up again, sweeping in off the sea, telling me it's time to go, make my way home, alone this time. There's a dark beauty in this change of mood, the shift to grey, a certain smug satisfaction that this place is mine in all its fickle aspects, as it was yours too. Belonging. I feel lighter somehow, a lift in the lower limbs, even though the incline is steep along the last lag to Channel View.

I turn the key in the front door; your hat is as it was, in its place, as though you might come along at any minute and place it on your head. I walk through to the conservatory, where we used to sit and chat and take in the view. It would be a great place to paint, you always told me. The purity of light. Once, only once, did you set up your easel there as I watched you, gentle brush stroke by gentle brush stroke, add the watery detail to make Burry Holms real. I'd asked you to paint the view from the window as a present for my husband's 60th birthday. You told me it was your favourite place on earth too, and when the time came, you'd like to be sprinkled there and for your earthly dust to be carried away on a puff of south-westerly breeze.

Here inside I feel safe, completely at home. I settle myself down on the settee, a sensation of calm coming over me, along with a sensation of company. Outside, the cumulus clouds are banking on the horizon over the sea, grey-bearded, unkempt, stray wisps and strands against fading blue. Overhead the herring gulls are squalling in a language I am beginning to understand. I unzip my backpack and take out the conch that's still there and clamp it tightly to my ear. Above the murmur of the waves and the strengthening wind, the message is clear and distinct. I open my laptop, make that incision in time, and commit a first sentence to the page.

THE SOUTH WESTERLIES

IT COMES AS news to me. As husband number two I don't know everything about her back story, especially when it comes to tables and chairs.

"It's the furniture I had when I was first married," she explains. "Daphne Atherton from up north, bought it along with the bungalow when we sold it. Then she sold the bungalow too, to buy this as a holiday home."

She's peering through the salt-caked sash-window, her left hand held to her temple in an attempt to see more. The sun is sinking into the ocean behind us, flooding the small square room on the other side of the glass with a deep pink glow. Inside, stands what looks like an oak refectory table with six ladder-back chairs, two at either side, and a carver at each end.

"What d'you, think?" she asks, "should we go for it?"

It's a beautiful place, I have to admit; and perhaps the furniture is telling us to buy this house together, in the village she's longed to return to for over thirty years.

"I used to babysit here a long time ago," she says as if almost to herself. "Always loved it. First house in the village to be built full-frontal to the ocean and not side-on. The south-westerlies."

By the time she has uttered this sentence, we have almost moved in without bothering to look around.

She has placed tapered candles in the pair of pewter holders: the wax is trickling down the metal and a diffuse tallow-light spreads through the room. The table is set for two: like a king and queen we take our places in the worn-armed carvers, facing each other across the elongated space. There is an ethereal quality about her and she exudes a calm that I have not felt before; sitting completely at ease on the frayed rush seat with its solid arms embracing her. I am uncomfortable in mine, as though there is someone filling the space with me. I feel I am about to be usurped. The physical distance between us is more than I'm used to, too formal somehow for a midweek supper.

Later, from the bedroom above, I'm sure I can hear the furniture crack and groan as it flexes its muscles, growing and stretching in the dark. It is as if her past is seeping out of the wood, oozing into the little front parlour, playing games with me in the dark.

&

In the morning, she's set the table again for breakfast. I watch her as she drinks her tea, stroking the surface of the old wood with her fingertips, tracing the grooves and the scratches and the knots absent-mindedly, as though the pull of the wood is dictating her actions. I wonder if any of the marks were made by her, back then, with him. Or even by him: the stab of a fork, the slice of a stainless-steel knife, the spill of Liebfraumilch, or even boiling water. But I don't ask. We just eat and clear and wash-up in the newly-fitted kitchen with barely a word spoken.

Like a genie with a lamp, she polishes her rediscovered

treasure with a zeal I have not noticed before as if she is trying to conjure something up, reconnect with her past. I am ruffled by the way she cares for it: no more spray and wipe but soft cloths and Fiddes beeswax for fine furniture which she orders online. I watch her smother the oak with the precious wax, and work it deep into the wood with firm circular, loving movements. And then she buffs till the table-top takes on a shine you can almost see your face in.

"It needs to be nourished," she says, "can't let it dry out again. Has to breathe."

It is as though she gives the kiss of life to these relics of her past. When we sit down to eat I notice how the chair arms are somehow smoother and silkier, how the grain at the side of my place mat stands out in stark relief to the rest of the wood. Sometimes I think I see faces in the patterns as I used to in the wallpaper and curtains of my bedroom when I was a child. Sometimes I think I see his face, leering at me; though I've never seen a picture of him.

It's soon after that she wakes me in the middle of the night to ask me if I can smell Gitanes. *French cigarettes*, she says, *can you smell them? Blue, black and white packet with a Spanish gypsy woman playing a tambourine?* I've never been a smoker and wouldn't know the difference between Gitanes, whatever they are, and any other. I inhale deeply; but there is not the slightest whiff of tobacco, French or otherwise. I tell her that sometimes people can smell things in dreams – the olfactory sense is very evocative – and not to worry. She accepts this and goes back to sleep. But in the nights that are to come there is a list of aromas and perfumes that I fail to smell: wood smoke, burnt toast, wet ashtrays, bad breath, Wrigley's spearmint gum, and night after night, Lux soap flakes and

Johnson's baby bath. And then the headaches start and she wears a sickly mask on her face.

I don't smell the smells she talks about; but I smell her. She's changed her perfume. When we kiss she tastes of iron filings and when she comes close, her breasts are full and heavy and slightly wet to the touch. But she won't let me inside her body; she can't risk it again, she says. She tells me she has not bled for three months, and that this time it will work out.

&

The MRI is clear. The pregnancy test is negative, despite the blood not flowing, the breasts engorging, the belly enlarging. The medical profession suggests it might be PTSD and asks whether there is anything she would like to talk to them about. They tell her that sometimes when people finally come out of a bad situation, and are secure and at their happiest, stress disorders re-emerge. The memory is a strange beast, and everyone deals with its imprints in different ways, they say.

"You're not happy with me, are you?" I blurt one night when we sit down to eat.

"Course I am," she says

"But look at you." She's gorging on yet another profiterole stack, the cream is oozing down her chin, and she's licking it up with the tip of her tongue.

"Don't go on," she says, wiping her lips on a napkin.

"Go on? You don't stop feeding your face, night after night. What's going on?"

But she says nothing, just places her knife and fork in the centre of her plate and pushes the plate to one side. Her chair scrapes against the flagstones as she gets up from the table.

"I'm going to bed," she says, "Heartburn. Being pregnant at my age takes it right out of you. Eating for two now."

"For Christ's sake, Nia," I shout, but then I decide against pursuing it, though have no inkling as to how this will resolve itself.

She looks straight through me. I listen to her groan as she strains to push the chair back in place as if already carrying a heavy load that I cannot see. I watch her waddle to the door, heavy-hipped and awkward. I remain sitting at the table until I think she has gone to sleep, though I feel that I am not alone.

❧

It's must be just after one when she shakes my shoulder.

"I can hear it again. It's not in my head, believe me," she pleads.

I don't know what would be better to believe her or not. But I show willing, sit up and switch on the bedside lamp.

"There . . . Hear it?" she whispers. "It's incessant. Thought it was a tomcat outside at first; but it's not stopping. Not going away. It's a baby. Know its cry. My flesh and blood. You must be able to hear it."

"No. Nothing," I reply.

"Downstairs. In the parlour."

"There's nothing, Nia. Try and shut whatever it is out and get some sleep."

She looks at me with a haunted hollow stare and I feel her slipping away from me like water through my palms. I watch her as she lumbers her body onto her left side and curls herself into a foetal position before she starts crying into the pillow.

Helpless at her side, I switch off the lamp after she has cried herself back to sleep, my hand gently rubbing the small of her back.

But sleep doesn't come to me. She has created demons in our dream house by the sea so I slip out of bed softly and go in search of a past which is poisoning the present. I creep onto the landing not daring to put on the light, expose my jealous weakness should she wake. I pad barefoot down the first set of seven stairs, pausing on the first dog-leg to check the time on the grandmother clock. Two a.m. I swiftly descend the bottom seven treads and then sidle along the passage to the front of the house and slink into the parlour.

The moon is suspended over the ocean out front, like a silver orb, throwing its milky whiteness into the room, illuminating the surface of the table. I sit in my pyjamas in the carver at the head of the table and it feels less like my place than ever. I sit in the glittering silence and will for something to reveal itself to me: for things that are not there to make me understand.

Though I've never seen a picture of him, his presence fills the room, the weight of him trying to force me out of my chair. For a minute, I think I'll succumb and vacate my position but then I hold out, lean back into it, stretching my legs straight out in front and crossing my arms, the way I used to sit in board rooms sometimes. I sense my body expand, filling the space, squeezing him out. Though he doesn't go. I hear him striding across the floor, the grate of wood on flags as he settles himself into the carver at the opposite end of the table. I can't distinguish a form or a face as much as I want to conjure them up; but I hear the rasp of a match being struck, see the glow from the tip of a cigarette. And then the room is filled with the choke of a tobacco I've never smelled before. I close my eyes and feel compelled to inhale.

How long I sit like this, I don't know. But long enough for me to wake from the reverie sleep-chilled. She's at the door. In the moonlight, her puffed up face takes on an aspect of the grotesque, as pale as the flimsy cotton nightie she is wearing that can't fail to shroud her bloated body. Eerily framed in the doorway, I realise she is nothing like the woman I married a few months earlier: There is something in her eyes that is fixated on something beyond me, nothing to do with me. I fear that she might burst.

"I smelled cigarettes again," she says, "Gitanes."

"God, Nia, why are you torturing yourself? Us?" I ask.

She shuffles towards me and strokes my hair. I place my hand over hers but find it difficult to raise my head, to look at her in the face. I hear her walk slowly to the other end of the table and then there's the slide of a drawer, wood on wood, the smooth glide of the runners. I lift my head. She reaches far into the back of this dark space and pulls out something small which I can't make out. She places her secret on the table top. In the frosty light, I can see that they are NHS hospital identity bracelets. They look lost and fragile against the solidity of the vast oak surface. I can see there are two bracelets: one much smaller than the other, though they are interlinked. The sight of the wristbands with the faded ink markings makes me feel like retching.

"I never knew," I say, holding her hand.

"Never talked about it. Things were different back then."

"Is that why you split up?" I ask.

"Always came between us. A big black hole," she says.

And she places her hand over the fabric covering her

growing abdomen and rubs gently in soft circular motions.

I get up from the table. She leads, with her stolen past cradled in her hands and me following in a kind of reverence. We leave the room and go out through the front door. The moon seems to be looking down and smiling sadly on us. Even the air is as still as death. I support my empty wife by the arm as we pick our way to the wild side of the garden, her clutching her precious memory close to her breasts. The transparent plastic with the ordinary white paper beneath seems to transform into brilliant white halos under the moon's radiance.

We come to rest where the grass is damp under the birches and I dig a trench, her standing silent just watching me. She inches forward and places the bands safe beneath the wet earth. *There*, she says. And then I shovel the freshly-dug soil back and place the silver-green and glistening turf back on top.

There is madness in the air, we can feel it; but together we feel completely sane.

"Are you sure?" I ask.

"Sure," she says. "Full of worms. Never keep it at bay."

We go back into the house to the front room. She takes one end and on the count of three we lift and manoeuvre the mock-Tudor table through the doorway and out into the night. We pick up a chair each and one-by-one we take all six and stack them at the side of the table in the middle of the front lawn. This time, it's an axe I fetch from the shed. I swing it hard into the timber, each stroke cutting deeper and deeper until the table and chairs are without form, a shapeless heap of debris, no more than desiccated sticks.

"Do you want to do it, or shall I?" she asks.

"I'll have great pleasure," I say.

I strike the match along the sandpaper edge of the box. The stench of phosphorous fills the air. We can both smell it. We breathe it in. I light yesterday's newspapers that we've crumpled into balls and placed under the kindling. We stand back, her head on my shoulder and gaze at the fire as it takes hold, crackling andgorging itself on the wood-feast. We watch transfixed as the burn continues and the flames lick the darkness, turning from crimson to orange to pale yellow to pure white, our faces warm and pink in the light of the inferno. And in the morning, the ash will rise, spiralling high into the sky and blow away on the south-westerlies.

GLOSSARY

Coffer bach – Welsh miniature chest traditionally given by husband to bride on wedding day

Melin Tregwynt – literally 'mill of the windy town' but known throughout the UK as the brand name of a very exclusive made in Wales woollen blanket

Bodalaw – 'bod' place + 'alaw' melody = place of melody

Calan Gaeaf – Hallowe'en

Mynd drot drot ar y gaseg wen
Mynd drot drot i'r dre
Mam yn dod 'nôl dros fryn a dôl
A rhywbeth neis neis i de

Go trot trot on the white horse
go trot trot to the town
Mum's coming back over hill and dale
with something nice nice for tea.

ACKNOWLEDGEMENTS

I WISH TO thank my many friends who make up a generous, world-wide community of writers. Each of them has played a part in my journey towards publication of *The South Westerlies*: Claire Keegan, Fflur Dafydd, Jon Gower, Rebecca F. John, Ellie Rees, John Lavin, Alan Bilton and the Hay Writers at Work cohort 2018. Their support has been both inspirational and invaluable. I also need to thank Chris and Jen Hamilton-Emery, and Nicholas Royle of Salt, for giving emerging writers like me a platform, and investing in the wonderful genre that is the short story.

NEW FICTION FROM SALT

ELEANOR ANSTRUTHER
A Perfect Explanation (978-1-78463-164-2)

NEIL CAMPBELL
Lanyards (978-1-78463-170-3)

MARK CAREW
Magnus (978-1-78463-204-5)

ANDREW COWAN
Your Fault (978-1-78463-180-2)

AMANTHI HARRIS
Beautiful Place (978-1-78463-193-2)

S. A. HARRIS
Haverscroft (978-1-78463-200-7)

CHRISTINA JAMES
Chasing Hares (978-1-78463-189-5)

NEW FICTION FROM SALT

VESNA MAIN
Good Day? (978-1-78463-191-8)

SIMON OKOTIE
After Absalon (978-1-78463-166-6)

TREVOR MARK THOMAS
The Bothy (978-1-78463-160-4)

TIM VINE
The Electric Dwarf (978-1-78463-172-7)

MICHAEL WALTERS
The Complex (978-1-78463-162-8)

GUY WARE
The Faculty of Indifference (978-1-78463-176-5)

MEIKE ZIERVOGEL
Flotsam (978-1-78463-178-9)

This book has been typeset by SALT PUBLISHING
LIMITED using Neacademia, a font designed by Sergei
Egorov for the Rosetta Type Foundry in the Czech
Republic. It is manufactured using Creamy 70gsm, a
Forest Stewardship Council™ certified paper from Stora
Enso's Anjala Mill in Finland. It was printed and bound
by Clays Limited in Bungay, Suffolk, Great Britain.

LONDON
GREAT BRITAIN
MMXIX